PATRICK CAUGHT HER BY THE SHOULDER. "YOU amaze me."

"I thought I mystified you," she said, her words whispering over him like erotic sensations.

He smiled. Slowly and gently, he drew her forward into the heat and strength of his body. Desire flowed into his bloodstream like a molten river. "That too. Am I making you nervous?"

She planted both her hands against his chest to maintain the space that separated their bodies. "Don't be silly."

"I'm not letting go of you."

She went absolutely still in his arms. "You aren't behaving normally," she accused.

"Restraint probably isn't normal, now that you mention it," he mused thoughtfully.

She looked up at him. "Why are you restraining yourself?"

"You aren't ready."

"You're wrong."

Startled by her matter-of-fact tone, he peered down at her. "Say that again, please."

She reached up, slid her arms around his neck, and then brought his head down. With her lips only a few inches from his, she whispered, "You're wrong, Patrick Matthew Sutton. You couldn't be more wrong. I *am* ready."

"Thank you, God," he muttered before he hungrily claimed her lips. . . .

WHAT ARE *LOVESWEPT* ROMANCES?

They are stories of true romance and touching emotion. We believe those two very important ingredients are constants in our highly sensual and very believable stories in the LOVE-SWEPT line. Our goal is to give you, the reader, stories of consistently high quality that may sometimes make you laugh, sometimes make you cry, but are always fresh and creative and contain many delightful surprises within their pages.

Most romance fans read an enormous number of books. Those they truly love, they keep. Others may be traded with friends and soon forgotten. We hope that each LOVESWEPT romance will be a treasure—a "keeper." We will always try to publish

LOVE STORIES YOU'LL NEVER FORGET
BY AUTHORS YOU'LL ALWAYS REMEMBER

The Editors

Loveswept 903

SMOKE AND MIRRORS

LAURA TAYLOR

BANTAM BOOKS
NEW YORK · TORONTO · LONDON · SYDNEY · AUCKLAND

SMOKE AND MIRRORS

A Bantam Book / September 1998

ISBN 0-553-44714-9

Published simultaneously in the United States and Canada

*Bantam Books are published by Bantam Books, a division of Bantam Dou-
bleday Dell Publishing Group, Inc. Its trademark, consisting of the words
"Bantam Books" and the portrayal of a rooster, is Registered in U.S.
Patent and Trademark Office and in other countries. Marca Registrada.
Bantam Books, 1540 Broadway, New York, New York 10036.*

PRINTED IN THE UNITED STATES OF AMERICA

OPM   10 9 8 7 6 5 4 3 2 1

This one is for Marla Miller Mazura,
friend, confidante, and talented
author; her husband, Terry Mazura;
and their beautiful daughters,
Jenna, Alivia, and Jessica.

I would like to acknowledge the technical
guidance I received from longtime friends
Georgette and Rick Hoffman,
of Rick Hoffman and Associates,
Consulting Engineering Geologists,
in Santa Barbara, California.
The errors are all mine!

ONE

Bailey Kincaid carefully navigated the rutted dirt road that wound through the foothills overlooking Santa Barbara. Once she reached the clearing, she guided her Jeep into position beside several parked trucks.

She automatically reached for her hard hat, the battered piece of headgear as much a part of her daily attire as her black twill jumpsuit and sturdy leather boots. Jamming the hard hat over the carelessly arranged knot of waist-length, white-gold hair that topped her head, she pushed open the door and exited her Jeep.

Bailey scanned the rough terrain as she approached the men waiting for her, her vivid blue eyes shielded behind a pair of sunglasses. When she spotted the condition of the water-well drilling site, she squared her shoulders. She also summoned what little patience she still possessed as she traversed the property known as Fox Ridge.

An idle job site was an annoyance to the co-owner and president of Kincaid Drilling; the fact that someone was deliberately sabotaging one of her jobs infuriated her. It wasn't the first time at this particular location, but she vowed that it would be the last.

Pete Higgins, the burly foreman, stepped away from the group of waiting men. He met Bailey as she paused at the edge of the mud-ringed drilling site. She noted his agitation, but she knew it wasn't in his nature to lose his temper even when things went awry.

"Was anyone injured?" she asked quietly.

"We lucked out, boss. When Manny cranked things up, we had pipe flying every which way. Everybody dove for cover, but someone coulda been killed."

She held on to her temper with both hands as she looked past Pete. The evidence of what had happened was right in front of her, but she found it difficult to come to terms with the costly and potentially deadly destruction. "Someone actually tampered with the top head drive on the tower of the drilling rig?"

Pete nodded. "It'll take a few days to get things back on track, provided we can get the new pipe and other replacement parts. I'll go by the shop when we're finished here and check our inventory, but I'm pretty sure I'm going to have to call the supplier in Enid," he said.

Bailey nodded. "Thanks, Pete." Removing her sunglasses, she studied the man who'd been like an uncle to her since her toddler days. "Why?"

"I wish I knew. I can only assume that somebody's real serious about not wanting this well to happen, which means the county won't allow the owner to move forward into the building phase."

Bailey nodded. "I'm getting the same impression, but I still don't understand why. The contractor's one of the most honest guys in the county, and I've seen all the permits, so I know everything's in order." Exhaling her irritation in a hard gust of air, she parked her shades back on the bridge of her nose. "Anything else I need to know?"

"You know what I know, boss, and it adds up to problems. My helpers are real edgy right now." Pete scratched his bald head. "Me, too, truth be told."

"All right, then. Clean up as best you can, secure the site, and then split your people between the Hastings project in Montecito and the Summerland job for the next day or so. Tell Manny and the rest of the guys that I appreciate their loyalty. Let me know when you get to the shop, and we'll figure out our next move."

Pete nodded, the expression on his craggy face assuring her that he knew she would do everything in her power to safeguard her employees. "Should I call Jeff and give him a heads-up?" he asked.

"No, I'll do it, but thanks for volunteering. He's been a real bear lately. Although big brother's already got enough on his plate at the police department, we need to meet face-to-face on this situation." Bailey saw Charlie Cannon wave a greeting in her direction as he chatted with Pete's drilling crew. She nodded, then refocused on Pete. "First, though, I guess I'd better have a talk with our favorite contractor."

"He's next in line, boss." Pete idly slapped his leather gloves against his thigh. "Anything else you need from me?"

Bailey cracked her first smile since getting the call from Pete an hour earlier. "When I was little, I used to come to you for hugs if Dad wasn't around. I think I might need one before this day is over," she teased.

She already felt the stress of having worked several eighteen-hour days in a row. The price of success, she knew, just as she knew better than to complain since she was in a feast-or-famine kind of business.

Settling a bear-sized paw on her slender shoulder, Pete chuckled as he peered down at her. "Me and Georgie are barbecuing tonight. Why don't you stop by and have supper with us? By the look of you, you've been missing too many meals lately."

She grinned. "I always look like a beanpole when I wear black."

Pete sobered. "You look beautiful to these old eyes, Miss Bailey Anne Kincaid. That ain't never gonna change, young lady." He tapped the tip of her nose with a single fingertip, the affectionate gesture a familiar one, then turned and lumbered back to his men.

Bailey mentally cataloged the condition of the drilling site in the minutes that followed. Her gaze traveled from the twisted lengths of pipe stacked nearby to the strips of red plastic ribbon tied to various pieces of equipment. The latter was Pete's way of marking equipment that needed repairs or replacement. But this time the red plastic ribbon also meant deliberate and potentially deadly vandalism that sent a chill across her soul.

Bailey decided to stop by the police department before she returned to her office. As senior homicide detective and acting chief at present, Jeff wouldn't handle a vandalism case. But as co-owner of Kincaid Drilling, he needed an immediate update on what had taken place.

Although she disliked the idea of going on the record about the vandalism, Bailey knew it was time to file a formal police report. The previous two episodes at the drilling site had been more of a nuisance than anything else. She'd avoided filing reports to protect the reputation of Kincaid Drilling and to keep a lid on their insurance premiums. This time, however, the repairs and replacement parts would be costly and the insurance company would require the documentation before processing her claim.

Charlie Cannon, the contractor responsible for

overseeing the development of the exclusive acreage that boasted a panoramic view of the Pacific Ocean for one of his Los Angeles clients, joined Bailey at the muddy perimeter of the drilling site. She saw and shared his obvious confusion over this latest effort to sabotage one of their jobs.

"I'm having a real hard time believing this, Bailey," he remarked. "You pay top wages, Kincaid Drilling has an excellent reputation across the state, and your safety record's the best around. I don't have any enemies I know of, and you don't either. What the heck do you make of this?"

She shrugged and nibbled on her lower lip before commenting, "At first I thought it was just a gang of bored teenagers making mischief. Then I thought it might be some environmental group, but now I don't think so. They usually give us some kind of a warning if we're stepping on their toes. Besides, the court system is far too friendly to their causes for them to have to resort to these tactics. Somebody's obviously got an ax to grind, and we need to figure out who and why."

"I'll have to notify the owner if we're going to be held up for more than a couple of days. He's in a real hurry to break ground."

"I understand," Bailey said, not envying him that particular conversation. A not-so-wonderful thought crossed her mind. "What about the owner? Is he . . ." She shrugged, not bothering to complete the sentence.

Charlie shook his head, clearly understanding

her real question as they turned away from the well site and moved in the direction of their vehicles. "Sutton is one of the good guys, Bailey. Very successful, solid reputation, kind of a loner, and anxious to get settled up here."

She nodded. "All right, then, I'll trust you."

"You can on this one. I've known him for several years. Our boys are fraternity brothers at UC Santa Barbara."

"I should talk to him," Bailey said, frustrated that such an encounter might be necessary. She liked dealing with the contractors, not their clients. Clients rarely understood the technical side of the well-drilling phase that preceded construction.

"I agree. Shall I set up a telephone conference call?" Charlie asked.

"Let's sort out this situation first," she suggested. "We don't have anything tangible to say to him other than the obvious, which is that we're experiencing a brief work stoppage."

He nodded. "All right. Shall I touch base with you later in the day?"

"Good idea."

Charlie glanced at his watch. "I need to check in with my office."

Bailey thought again of her older brother. "I have a call to make too."

Charlie paused at his truck. Bailey completed the steps to her Jeep. Reaching inside, she picked up her cellular phone and depressed a single button that dialed a preprogrammed number. It rang once before a masculine voice barked a greeting.

"Hi, Jeff. I need ten minutes this morning. We've got a vandalism problem with the job at Fox Ridge." She paused, winced when he let fly a graphic phrase guaranteed to make a dockworker blush, and then said, "Thanks. I'll be there in twenty or thirty minutes."

The sound of the dial tone gave way to the drone of car engines laboring up the winding dirt road and into the bulldozed clearing. Bailey glanced curiously at Charlie, who joined her as two stretch limousines pulled up less than ten feet in front of them.

The vehicles shouted Hollyweird, just like the collection of funkily attired men and women who piled out of the passenger doors. A cameraman, and what appeared to be an assistant who was loaded down like a pack mule with various pieces of camera gear, followed.

"Don't these people know that this is private property and not a movie set?" Bailey asked, her exasperation flaring because a film crew was the last thing she wanted or needed in her life. Now or ever, thanks to her past. She pivoted and started to reach for the door handle of her Jeep.

Charlie caught her arm before she could jerk open the door and climb in. "Don't run off. I'll introduce you."

"This isn't a good time for socializing, Charlie," she protested. She knew Charlie catered almost exclusively to the monied entertainment community that sought privacy in the Santa Barbara area.

Bailey frowned the instant she noticed the overly made-up and excessively coiffed middle-aged woman who pushed open a passenger door and exited one of the limos. The woman looked vaguely familiar, but Bailey didn't know why. She shook her head. She didn't have time for this.

Her thoughts scattered a few seconds later as she glanced at the open rear door of the second limo. A tall, dark-haired man unfolded himself from the interior of the vehicle. With his back to her, he straightened to a height of well over six feet.

Although she wasn't sure why, Bailey stiffened when he removed his sunglasses and slowly turned around. She felt as if she'd been slapped across the face when his gaze settled on her. Unwilling to believe her eyes at first, Bailey simply stared at him.

Charlie strode in the direction of their visitor, all smiles as he greeted him. "Patrick. It's great to see you, man."

Unable to budge as the two men shook hands, Bailey concentrated on steadying her respiration. Reminders of the past unsettled her, especially when they sent her hurtling back in time to an unfaithful husband and an emotionally devastating divorce.

Patrick Sutton. Her ex-husband's theatrical agent and business manager since the start of his acting career. For all she knew, he still played a critical role in Jeremy's life. She no longer cared one way or another. Whatever the connection between Patrick Sutton and Jeremy Strong, it was their business. Bailey wanted nothing to do with it. Or them.

In her opinion, Patrick Sutton was the kind of man who excelled in a place like Hollywood. He had been, and probably still was, a slick operator with the instincts of a piranha. She remembered him as ruthless to the core, ruthless enough to urge her to overlook the fact that Jeremy had felt compelled to test his manhood with everything in a skirt during their six-year marriage.

The fact that she'd also been drawn to Sutton in an alarmingly sensual manner had simply added insult to injury. It had also convinced her that she was at risk of becoming like the unethical types she'd grown to despise before ending her marriage and fleeing Los Angeles. She hadn't been back in five years. She had no plans to return. And she neither wanted nor needed any trips down memory lane that reminded her of the humiliation she'd endured or made her feel as though her morals were in jeopardy.

Sutton's gaze drifted past her. Shaken, Bailey breathed a shallow sigh of relief and told herself to straighten up. She weighed twenty pounds less than when they last met, her jumpsuit and hard hat were a far cry from the revealing wardrobe she'd reluctantly worn to please her ex-husband, and she'd reclaimed her family name after the divorce. She decided that Sutton probably wouldn't ever remember her, but she said a quick prayer to guarantee it.

When Charlie turned and motioned her forward, Bailey found her gumption and her voice. "I've got an appointment, so we'll have to save this for later."

Charlie behaved as though he'd suddenly developed a hearing impairment. "Patrick Sutton, come on over here and meet the resident geologist and president of Kincaid Drilling, Bailey Kincaid. Her people are handling your water."

Sutton was still too attractive for any woman's peace of mind, Bailey concluded as the two men paused in front of her. He moved with the innate grace of a powerful and very predatory jungle cat.

Good manners ingrained during her childhood kept Bailey from turning on her heel and walking away when Patrick Sutton extended his hand in greeting. She reluctantly accepted it, shook it, and then freed herself of his touch as quickly as possible. Stepping backward until the solid bulk of her Jeep forced her to halt her retreat, she considered the space she put between them critical to her composure.

He half smiled. "Good morning, Miss Kincaid. Beautiful day, isn't it?"

Without understanding precisely why, she resented the unruffled expression etched into his hard-featured face. She gripped her cell phone with both hands as she looked at him.

After he scanned the idle work crew and the closed-down drilling site, Patrick Sutton's smile faded as he returned his gaze to Bailey. "Is there a problem?"

He spoke in a tone of voice so low and so intimate that she felt like the only other person on the planet. Bailey belatedly realized that she wasn't even sure what he'd just said to her.

Her anxiety escalated. Bailey recalled being entranced by his voice at a particularly vulnerable time in her life. She'd forgotten the power of the sound. She resolved not to forget it again or to respond to it. Not now. Not ever.

She also remembered her struggle not to react to Patrick Sutton in other ways during her years in Los Angeles. She'd never allowed him to seduce her body, but he had seduced her emotions and her senses, thanks to his sensuality, his confidence, and his apparent certainty that he had a right to the power he wielded. She'd desired him in such an intensely reckless way that it had frightened her.

"Miss Kincaid, is there a problem?" Patrick questioned a second time.

She heard the words this time, but the cameraman suddenly darted in her direction, his camera trained on her. Caught off guard, Bailey flinched. "Is this necessary?" she asked as she cast an annoyed look at the man.

Sutton glanced at the cameraman. "Tommy, let's give the lady a break. She's a civilian, after all."

Much to her relief, Tommy backed off and shifted his focus to the varied terrain of Fox Ridge.

"I apologize, Miss Kincaid. Tommy is shooting a documentary for PBS, and his enthusiasm sometimes gets in the way of his common sense." Patrick smiled. "Unfortunately, I agreed to be one of his profile subjects before I realized how intrusive the process could be."

Please, don't be nice, she thought.

Charlie Cannon said, "Bailey, I'd like you to fill Patrick in on the—"

She held up her hand, glancing in the direction of the cameraman, who had turned his attention and his camera on them yet again. "I think it would probably be best to . . ." she began, then glared at the documentary filmmaker when he started to advance on her.

Did she really want to suggest a private meeting? Bailey couldn't help wondering. She exhaled, the sound one of defeat. She had no other choice and she knew it.

Patrick Sutton's gaze traveled from the contractor to Bailey, then lingered on her. "We need a meeting, don't we?"

As she nodded Bailey had the impression that he was trying to see beyond the sunglasses that shielded a good portion of her face from view.

As he moved a step closer to her he added, "And in a less public place, I suspect."

Bailey inclined her head, acknowledging his grasp of the situation. "Would this afternoon be convenient?" As she voiced the question she comforted herself with the realization that Charlie would make a great buffer if Sutton remembered her as Jeremy Strong's ex-wife during a meeting that she planned to keep very short.

The big-haired woman hovering nearby inserted herself into the conversation. "Patrick, your schedule is ironclad for the next few hours, but I can arrange a thirty-minute opening at two."

Sutton's focus remained on Bailey. "Thanks, Jeanne."

Bailey controlled her surprise, although it took a concerted effort. She hadn't recognized Jeanne Carson, who had aged none too gracefully in recent years. Given her appearance, Bailey couldn't help wondering if she'd experienced, and had yet to recover from, a personal crisis or a difficult health problem.

As Patrick Sutton's longtime executive assistant, she had always been a very powerful force at the Sutton Group. Jeremy had sung Jeanne's praises, but Bailey had never been able to warm to the woman. She'd always seemed brittle and far too calculating to trust, but then so had everyone and everything else in the land of smoke and mirrors.

"Where shall we meet?" Patrick Sutton asked.

Bailey glanced at Charlie. "Your office is centrally located."

He looked confused. "Did you forget we're under construction? Your place makes more sense."

She had forgotten, much to her chagrin. Bailey

extracted a business card from her jumpsuit pocket and handed it to Patrick Sutton. "My office? Two o'clock?"

"Two is good for me," Charlie Cannon announced, his usual relaxed smile reappearing.

"I'll be there," Sutton said, his facial expression intent as he pocketed her business card.

"I'm not far from the Mission."

"I know the area." Sutton reached around her and pulled open the driver's-side door to the Jeep.

Bailey brushed against him as she climbed into the vehicle. Her heart rate instantly accelerated. Settling quickly in her seat, she reached out to pull the door closed, but she hesitated when she realized that Patrick Sutton had a firm grip on it.

"Are you all right?" he asked.

His question startled her. As she formed a reply and resisted the allure of his low voice, Bailey noted that Charlie Cannon and Jeanne Carson had their heads together and were wandering in the direction of the drilling site.

"You haven't answered me," Sutton remarked, his long-fingered hand still on the door.

Bailey fastened her seat belt before meeting his direct gaze. "Of course I'm all right. I just have a lot on my mind at the moment."

Although he nodded, she sensed that he was on the verge of contradicting her. He closed the Jeep's door, instead. Bailey exhaled shallowly.

"I noticed the damage to the drilling rig and the

stacked lengths of pipe," he said through the open window.

She lowered her hands to her lap and pressed her palms together. "And?"

"And I grew up in West Texas."

The absence of a telltale accent made his announcement that much more of a surprise. She told herself not to be surprised in the next instant. She'd long ago concluded that Patrick Sutton was part chameleon. "Then you've probably got a good idea about what's happened."

"I suspect so," he conceded.

"Then perhaps a meeting is unnecessary," Bailey commented, wondering about his real agenda. Her heart sank a little. Maybe he'd recognized her, after all.

"I don't consider talking a waste of time."

"Talking isn't wasted if the conversation is relevant," she pointed out with as much composure as she could manage. Heat flushed her cheeks. It was definitely time to make a graceful exit, she decided. "I'm late for an appointment, so please excuse me."

He stepped back from the Jeep. "Drive carefully, Miss Kincaid."

"I always do, Mr. Sutton."

"I hope so."

She turned the key in the ignition. "Trust me, I do."

"I do trust you, and there's no reason for you not to trust me."

She paled as she looked at him. "Excuse me?"

He smiled. "You heard me."

How could I ever trust you? she wondered. Bailey released the brake and seized the gearshift knob. "Have a nice day."

"I always try to," he remarked.

She shifted into first and started to guide the Jeep out of the clearing. Despite the impulse to look at him one last time, Bailey managed not to glance in the rearview mirror as she departed Fox Ridge.

By the time she reached the end of the dirt road that snaked through Sutton's densely wooded property, she felt more foolish than she had in a very long time. Her next encounter with Patrick Sutton, she promised herself, would be short and to the point. At thirty-three years of age, Bailey Kincaid knew better than to tempt fate by lingering in the company of a man who made her feel as though her common sense had taken an extended vacation, a man who aroused her cravings for things best left to the imagination.

TWO

The smile easing the hard angles of Patrick Sutton's face disappeared as he watched Bailey leave. And as he watched he wondered why she'd pretended that they were strangers.

Grateful that his companions had wandered off to explore the Fox Ridge acreage, Patrick gave himself time to deal with the shock he felt at seeing her again after five years. He unclenched his fists, pressing his palms against his thighs.

He'd recognized her immediately, despite the obvious changes in her appearance. As his heart rate slowed to a gallop he realized what it had cost him to restrain an almost overwhelming urge to reach out and touch her. If only to reassure himself that she was real and not some figment produced by his imagination.

Bailey Kincaid Strong. Patrick shook his head in amazement. He'd never forgotten her. Never.

She'd lived on the periphery of his mind, a private fantasy sustained by emotions and needs too diverse to itemize.

He'd never known anyone like her. Her ex-husband had never gotten the point that Bailey was the kind of woman who was meant to be appreciated and cherished. At first the actor had simply taken her for granted. In the end, though, he'd lost a very unique woman to a combination of carelessness and outright stupidity.

Patrick hadn't expected to see Bailey again. He hadn't wanted to add to her pain, so he'd left her alone.

His respect for her had held him at bay, and he'd kept his feelings for her under wraps, despite the cost to himself. He knew that she'd never guessed the extent of his regard and desire for her. She'd been too earnest and innocent when they'd first met. By the time her marriage had ended, she'd been far too wounded to trust another man.

Patrick Sutton rarely found himself thrown off balance by people or life, but the feeling persisted. Bailey had always done that to him, he recalled. Oddly, he hadn't minded in the past, and he discovered that he really didn't mind now.

He chuckled ruefully at himself, aware that he possessed a reputation of being a calculating predator. In point of fact, he was a powerful man who successfully managed the careers and business affairs of an elite group of world-class actors.

His client list was short. His choice. The list

was exclusive. His choice again. And the list wouldn't ever undergo expansion. His choice as well.

Patrick knew that by anyone's standards, he was a success. He never questioned that fact or the instincts that guided him. His intellect, his personality, and his negotiating talent allowed him to march to his own drummer. He trusted those character traits, because he knew his own strengths. He also knew his weaknesses, but he resisted them—just as he'd resisted his hunger for Bailey—with an innate strength that kept him from falling prey to them when fatigue or frustration or loneliness set in.

He liked himself, which often surprised people when they realized it. Some of those same people perceived him as egotistical. He conceded that he probably was, but he rarely worried about other people's perceptions of him.

His priorities were firmly fixed. He cared deeply about his college-age son—the son he'd raised following his wife's unexpected death from medical complications during childbirth. And he cared about the two other issues that currently dominated his world: the peace of mind he'd recently lost and his desire to alter the course of his life. Both presented a challenge, and by realizing the second, he hoped to regain the first.

Patrick thrived on challenge and change. He considered life too fluid and the world too capricious to behave in any other manner. That someone was intent on destroying all that he'd built angered him, but he dealt with that nameless, faceless entity like any power broker worth his salt. He controlled his anger, and he waited. The man who had brought more than one studio head to his knees on behalf of a client vowed to emerge triumphant. He refused to accept any other outcome.

Determination evident in his long-legged stride, Patrick turned and walked the short distance to the disabled water-well drilling rig. His thoughts remained concealed behind a neutral expression as he surveyed the site.

Patrick wanted to reject the notion that the person responsible for the vandalism in Beverly Hills had followed him there, but he knew he couldn't completely discount the possibility. The founder and driving force of the Sutton Group whispered a silent prayer that the damage to the drilling rig was just a terrible coincidence.

"Patrick?"

He glanced at his executive assistant as she tucked her cell phone into her leather satchel and paused at his side. "What is it, Jeanne?"

"Mal Holcomb is up here scouting movie locations. He wants to see you, so I've rearranged your afternoon schedule accordingly."

Patrick nodded. An Oscar-caliber director and close friend, Mal was a priority under normal circumstances. The fact that two Sutton Group clients were in rehearsal for his next film prompted Patrick to accommodate him even more readily. "Any specific problems with the film?" he asked.

"I honestly don't know. Mal was vague, which isn't his usual style," she commented.

Patrick frowned. "You're right, it isn't. He's a brilliant director, but sometimes I think he has a secret desire to become a drill instructor in his next life."

"Or maybe a pit bull." Jeanne rolled her eyes. "We've got a scheduling conflict, but I can fit Miss Kincaid into a later slot at the end of the workday, if she's willing to cooperate."

"Give her a call, please, but with an apology for the inconvenience. And speak to her yourself, if possible."

Jeanne pursed her lips, her humor fading. "Flowers too?"

"Not a great idea," he said, recalling a comment that Bailey had once made about gratuitous gestures being typically Hollywood.

"Perhaps a new tool belt?" Jeanne suggested, her tone faintly sarcastic.

Patrick ignored the sarcasm. "Just convey my apologies when you talk to her, and reschedule for another time this afternoon."

Jeanne bristled visibly. "My ears work."

Patrick ignored her prickly response. He knew she disliked being given instructions on how to do her job. He normally didn't, because she took her responsibilities seriously and rarely, if ever, failed to meet them. But he wanted Bailey Kincaid handled with kid gloves. "Anything else?" he asked.

She shot a glance in the direction of the far edge of the clearing. "Tommy's waiting on you."

He nodded, his expression reluctant. "Lucky me."

"Now what's the matter?" Jeanne asked.

Patrick smiled, accustomed to her directness. They'd been friends for a long time, so he didn't consider her question intrusive. "Just thinking."

"Not good thoughts, by the look on your face."

Patrick shrugged dismissively, then squared his broad shoulders. He regretted ever agreeing to Tommy's request that he participate in a documentary about behind-the-scenes power in Hollywood. He missed his privacy. He craved it in the same way that some people craved their morning jolt of caffeine.

"Anything your intrepid assistant can handle for you?"

He slid his arm around her stocky body and gave her a warm hug. "Not a thing, but thanks for offering." Shifting his hand to her elbow, he guided her across the uneven terrain. "Let's deal with Tommy."

"Smart man," she said, her features softening as she glanced at Patrick.

"I've had just about enough of our award-winning film genius."

Jeanne laughed. "You're the one who gave him carte blanche."

"Don't remind me."

"He thinks you're fascinating, so take your bows like a good trouper."

"I'm fed up to the teeth with Tommy and his entourage as my permanent shadow."

"When he films you sleeping, you'll know you're in real trouble."

Patrick chuckled. "He tried that last week on the London flight. I almost tossed him out of the plane before we began our descent into Heathrow."

Her expression turned serious. "You've got a lot on your plate over the next few weeks, and we don't need him underfoot."

"I know. I'm going to have to revoke his carte blanche."

"Why don't you let me deal with him?" she suggested. "That's part of my job description, anyway."

"Playing resident cop?" Patrick teased.

"I'll play resident-anything-I-need-to-be in order to take care of you, and don't you forget it," Jeanne counseled, a faint smile blunting her terse tone.

"Not a chance. I bow to your job description and all that it entails. With gratitude. We both know I'd be lost without you."

He released her arm as Tommy swung around and marched on them with his camera raised. Patrick muttered a dark word, then got his irritation under control in short order before glancing back at Jeanne. "Don't forget to call Miss Kincaid. I really don't want her inconvenienced."

"You know I never forget anything, Patrick."

Jeanne Carson smiled at him then, a smile that was caught on film by the ever-vigilant Tommy before she turned away. The epitome of efficiency, she extracted her cell phone from her satchel, flipped it open, and punched out several numbers from memory.

Patrick endured another thirty minutes with Tommy Dunlap before Jeanne herded everyone back to the limos. As he was driven to his next appointment, sans Tommy and his entourage, he savored the quiet of the drive. His thoughts returned to Bailey, and he realized that one of the things he'd missed most about her was the sound of her laughter. He couldn't help wondering if he would ever hear it again.

Seated at her desk as dusk enveloped the community in a gentle embrace, Bailey reviewed the insurance-claim forms she'd spent the afternoon completing for the Fox Ridge job. She heard the tinkling bell attached to the courtyard gate.

Expecting to see Jeff, who often stopped in to say hello when he had the time, she shifted her gaze to the unobstructed glass panes of the French doors. Beyond the doors was a spacious tiled courtyard filled with flowering rosebushes and plump ferns.

Her annoyance spiked when Patrick Sutton stepped into view. He was several hours late for their appointment. Her employees had left for the day, and Charlie Cannon had long since departed, pleading an engagement with his wife and children.

Bailey pushed up from her desk and crossed the room, pausing in front of the French doors. She felt on edge about the prospect of dealing with Patrick Sutton. As she pulled open the double doors she felt the force of the desire that the mere sight of him inspired.

"Thanks for waiting for me," he said by way of a greeting.

Bailey inclined her head, but she didn't say anything. She longed to read him the riot act for assuming that she had nothing better to do than sit around twiddling her thumbs while he fit her into his schedule. Instead, she led the way into her office and returned to the chair behind her desk.

Patrick followed her, sinking into one of the chairs positioned in front of her antique oak desk. "Long day," he commented.

"It happens." She kept her voice even, her expression level. He looked tired. Compassion blossomed inside her, but she controlled the emotion. Their meeting was about business. Nothing else.

Patrick glanced around the spacious office. "Great house."

"Thank you."

"I've always liked Mission-style architecture."

"It's very comfortable."

"Did you grow up here? In this house, I mean."

"Yes." Although she didn't offer the information, the conversion of the main house to office space for Kincaid Drilling had taken place after her father's death and her mother's remarriage and subsequent move to San Francisco. Bailey lived in one of two cottages situated on the property. Her brother resided in the other one.

Patrick smiled. "The trees that line the perimeter of the property are spectacular. I have a mental image of a little girl with long braids and a sunburned nose clambering around in her tree house. The acreage appears to occupy a full residential block."

"It does, so we've allowed the foliage to do its own thing."

"We?" Patrick said ever so softly.

His gaze fell to her ringless left hand, then shifted up to her face. "Your husband?"

"My brother, Jeff." This was getting too personal, a voice in her head commented. She flattened her hands on the paperwork strewn across the top of her desk to remind herself of the damaged drilling rig.

As Patrick openly studied her she allowed herself a moment to wonder what he was seeing. She now felt certain that he remembered her, especially since she no longer wore her sunglasses and hard hat. Clad in a T-shirt and jeans, with her hair flowing unbound down her back to her waist like a schoolgirl's, she wished she hadn't changed out of her work clothes. She straightened in her chair. "You're staring, Mr. Sutton."

"You've lost weight since I last saw you, and your hair is a lot longer."

Bailey exhaled shallowly.

"You've changed in other ways, as well," he observed.

"And have you?" she asked quietly.

Patrick Sutton shrugged. "Maybe, maybe not."

"You probably haven't," she observed. "Most people don't, from what I can tell."

"Life's fluid." He smiled, but there was no real humor in his expression. "And your bias against anything connected to Hollywood is showing."

"I've never tried to hide it."

"No, you haven't, have you? You paid a very high price for your candor, though."

"Why didn't you say anything this afternoon?" she asked.

"It was obvious you didn't want me to."

"Why be so accommodating?"

"No special reason."

She cocked her head to one side, studying him intently. "No offense, but I find that hard to believe."

"Why?"

"I remember you as a man with numerous private agendas, Mr. Sutton."

"Patrick," he said.

She heard the edge in his voice. She'd annoyed him, she realized, but she didn't feel compelled to apologize. He needed to understand that she really was a different person now. "All right, Patrick, let's get to the point of your visit."

"Without Charlie?"

"He stayed as long as he could."

"And you had no other choice but to wait for me," he speculated.

"You're the client," she pointed out.

"And someone had to deal with me?"

"That's one way of putting it."

He laughed then. "You really have changed, haven't you?"

"I grew up."

"One of the hazards of navigating the world."

She inclined her head in agreement. "That's been my experience."

"You've done well for yourself, Bailey."

"People adapt, don't they?" Cruelty and betrayal had been the catalysts for the changes she'd undergone, but she had no desire to discuss the past with Patrick Sutton. "Why don't we get started? I assume you have questions."

"I do. How much of a delay are we talking about?"

"Probably seventy-two hours, provided our shipment arrives as promised."

"From Enid?"

He understood more about the drilling business than she had originally guessed. Bailey nodded. "The building boom has us operating at full tilt right now, so I'm stretched to the limit as far as machinery, replacement pipe, and personnel are concerned."

"I always thought you'd teach geology," Patrick remarked.

Startled that he recalled a conversation they'd once had about her plans for the future, she saw no gain in sidestepping his observation. "That was what I intended."

Things had changed, though, and she'd adjusted to reality. Her specialty, she realized. Adjusting to other people's actions. She did less of that now, much to her relief. Being in the driver's seat of her life suited her. And, someday, she would teach, because it was a dream she didn't intend to relinquish.

"What happened?" he asked quietly.

She felt unnerved by the kindness she heard in his low voice. Unnerved, as well, by the seductive undertone. "Does it matter?"

"I'm interested."

"Why?" she asked.

"I was always interested, Bailey, but you were too shy in those days to realize it."

"I was nothing more than excess baggage in Jeremy's life."

"What made you think that?"

The pain of those days, the feeling of never belonging in that group of self-absorbed creative types, returned tenfold and almost brought tears to her eyes. "The way you all tolerated me."

"You were a breath of fresh air."

She promptly countered, "I was a naive fool who trusted the wrong people."

"Hollyweird's a tough place," Patrick conceded.

A smile tugged at the edges of her lips. She couldn't stop it. So he remembered her derisive term for the land of make-believe. "It made mincemeat out of me," she conceded, some of her resentment and wariness displaced by his seemingly compassionate tone of voice.

"Don't feel singled out," Patrick advised.

"I did, at the time. Now I know better," she admitted. "That place gives new meaning to the phrase *survival of the fittest.*"

"A veritable jungle, despite all the image making that goes on," he said, surprising her by agreeing with her. "Now, tell me about the well site. What happens next?"

She gave him a direct look. "Perhaps nothing at all."

"Vandalism happens all the time. Any idea of the motivation?"

"None."

"How do you intend to handle it?"

"I intend to keep my people out of harm's way," she cautioned.

"And how do you propose to do that?" he asked in that measured quiet tone of his.

"By closing down the job site."

He studied her for a long moment. "Permanently?"

"I'm giving it serious consideration."

Patrick sank back in his chair, but he looked anything but relaxed. "Is that the advice given to you by the police, or is this a decision you'll reach on your own?"

"My bottom line is simple. I will not jeopardize my employees."

"I don't expect that of you, Bailey. And you haven't answered my question."

Again, she said, "I won't jeopardize my employees. And we both know that there are other water-well drillers in the area."

"I'm surprised," he said.

"By what?"

"I never thought you were a coward."

"Safety is the issue, not courage. And safety isn't for sale, not at any price."

"One bad experience, and you're bailing out?"

"This isn't the first incident."

Patrick abandoned his chair and strolled around the office, which had once served as a formal dining room. "Tell me about the other incidents, please."

Bailey watched him, her appreciation for the long lean lines of his body flaring to life inside her. Disgusted with her response, she forced herself beyond her sensory awareness of his maleness and sensuality. "Nuisance messes, for the most part. Nothing too costly to replace or fix, just annoying when you're already on a tight schedule and you have to waste time cleaning up."

He stopped prowling. "How many times?"

"Twice in the last four days. Someone could have been killed this morning."

"I understand your concern. It's the same concern that I feel for the people I employ."

She studied him for a long moment.

"Bailey, I do understand."

"How could you?" she asked almost fervently. "Your world disposes of people. It mashes and smashes them like a trash compactor. The men and women who work for Kincaid Drilling are my family."

Patrick massaged the back of his neck, then rolled his head from side to side. "One of these days it's going to occur to you that I'm not the enemy. I hope I'm around when it happens."

"This isn't about you, and it isn't about me. The simple truth is that I'm worried about the safety of my drilling foreman and his helpers," she insisted. She got to her feet, but she remained standing behind her desk. Her instincts assured her that getting too close to Patrick Sutton would be an error in judgment. A big one. "Who has a grudge against you?"

He shrugged. "No one that I'm aware of."

Something about the shuttered look that came over his face bothered her. "Why don't I believe you?"

"Do I need to remind you that it was your equipment that was targeted, Ms. Kincaid? Perhaps you should look to your own backyard. Does someone have a grudge against you?"

She shook her head, her mounting suspicion evident in the vivid blue of her eyes. "You're a more likely target, Mr. Sutton, especially given your celebrity status and the way people like you do business."

Patrick flinched. "It's easier for you to believe the worst of me, isn't it?"

Was it? she wondered, but only briefly. She promptly reminded herself that he'd been the one who'd tried to persuade her to overlook Jeremy's repeated episodes of infidelity. Patrick Sutton hadn't wanted his client upset by the possibility of divorce proceedings during auditions for the crucial film role that ultimately launched his acting career.

Priorities. It had been all about their priorities, she remembered. She'd been expendable. Learning that lesson had been the final blow to her love for Jeremy. It had also damaged her ability to trust.

Bailey exhaled shallowly. Drained by countless eighteen-hour workdays and by the raft of painful memories that Patrick Sutton symbolized, she shifted to her bottom line. "I'm giving some very serious thought to pulling my crew and withdrawing from the job. I'll call Charlie in the morning with my decision."

"I'm asking you not to."

"If your house means that much to you, then—"

He cut in, "A house is a building, but having a home means a great deal to me. Regardless of what you think of me, I don't want anyone injured or killed."

"Are you certain that the vandalism has nothing to do with you or the Sutton Group?"

"How can anyone be certain of something like that?" he asked.

She knew his question wasn't unreasonable, but she didn't like it. "That's not an answer, so you've made my decision for me. I'll have my accountant cut a refund check. You'll have it before the close of business on Friday."

He shook his head. "Don't do that."

"It's the right thing to do."

"I already know you're a moral woman, so there's no need to prove it to me."

She stared at him, uncertainty creeping into her mind and silencing her. She sensed then that something important was troubling him. Something more important than the success or failure of sinking a well at the Fox Ridge property. But what? she wondered, then promptly told herself that it didn't concern her.

"I've got an idea," he said a few moments later, catching her by surprise.

"I'm listening." But why was she even willing to listen to this man? Because she was certifiable, she concluded.

"Around-the-clock security at Fox Ridge, at my expense, of course, and a bonus if Kincaid Drilling completes the job."

The second half of his proposal contained the sting of a hard slap. "I'm not for sale."

"Relax, I'm not trying to buy you off."

"Then what exactly are you trying to do?"

"I wouldn't insult you that way. The bonus is for your employees. Call it hazard pay, if you'd like."

The impasse they'd just reached and her genuine weariness finally took their toll on her. Bailey massaged the bridge of her nose with her fingertips, then lowered her hand and met his gaze. "Look, I've had a very long day, and I need some sleep. Why don't you call Charlie Cannon first thing in the morning? Have him hire another drilling company. We'll chalk this situation up to experience, and you'll have a fresh start on the project. I'll even throw in all the hydro-geologic survey work I've done."

"Meet me halfway, Bailey."

Exasperated by his stubbornness, she asked the obvious question. "Why is this so important to you?"

"It's important," he said. "And I'm not trying to hustle you."

"Why?" she pressed.

"My future is here."

She blinked. The man was in his prime by Hollywood power-broker standards. "Are you retiring?"

He chuckled. "At forty-two? Hardly."

She paled as a disturbing thought crossed her

mind. She voiced it, unaware of the worry that underscored her next question. "Are you ill?"

"No."

"Then why Kincaid Drilling?"

"Because you're the best, or Charlie wouldn't have hired you."

"That's too simple, and, for the record, stroking my ego is a waste of time."

"What about the terms I've proposed, but on a day-to-day basis? Once you're ready to start up again, I'll absorb the operating and payroll costs if anything goes wrong."

"That's crazy!" she exclaimed.

He approached her desk, an assessing look in his gray eyes. She held her ground by the sheer force of her will, all the while reminding herself that he couldn't walk through the piece of furniture. Bailey knew she couldn't let him get near enough to touch her, however innocently. She sensed that she'd cave in if that happened.

"So call me crazy."

"You're crazy," she said, her tone passionate.

He laughed.

"Patrick, this is a bad idea. Jobs get jinxed."

Still smiling, he shook his head. "You're a geologist, not some superstitious creature from the fifteenth century."

"It happens. And I may be a geologist, but I'm also responsible for the welfare of people who depend on my common sense."

"So am I, and I understand the pressures, Bailey. I understand far better than you can imagine."

She studied him, trying to grasp where he was coming from. Unfortunately, she didn't have a clue.

"I meant it when I said you could trust me."

She shook her head. "You're asking a lot, Patrick. You of all people should understand why."

"I don't blame you for the way you feel, but what happened was between you and Jeremy. I wound up in the middle, which was the last place I wanted to be."

Bailey felt a chill move across her heart. "I have a very clear memory of the past and what happened."

"It's your memory," he reminded her. "A memory that is directly influenced by the humiliation you suffered at Jeremy's hands. I am not Jeremy Strong, and I'd appreciate it if you wouldn't forget that fact. If you feel the need to judge me, then do it based on what you learn firsthand about me, not on the actions of another man. I will not pay his penance for him, Bailey. Not now. Not ever."

He was right, but she refused to admit it aloud. She suddenly felt guilty for tarring and feathering him because of his association with her ex-husband. She had, though, she realized. And what kind of a person did that make her? Stupid? Vulnerable? Probably both, she concluded.

"Give some thought to what I'm proposing, why don't you? I'll call you in the morning."

She exhaled, pondering his proposal as they silently evaluated each other. She weighed safety against paranoia. She also weighed the wisdom of taking on the emotional risk that he posed. He was a huge risk, because she realized that she was still attracted to him. Probably more now than before, if that was even possible. He was a flame, and she felt like the proverbial moth, inexorably drawn to him, regardless of the jeopardy.

Bailey sighed. She closed her eyes against the sting of emotions that surged up inside her.

"What's wrong?" Patrick asked.

He seduced her with his voice, seduced her so thoroughly that she ached inside and forgot to guard her tongue. "You frighten me."

"That's not my intent, Bailey. It never was, and it never will be. I promise you. I wouldn't harm you for the world."

Startled and confused by his intensity, she blinked away the tears swimming in her eyes and refocused on him. "What we intend isn't always what happens."

"You're right. A long time ago I tried to keep you out of harm's way, but I failed. The damage that was done to you was inexcusable, but I counted on your strength of character to get you through the crisis. I see now that I wasn't wrong about you. You're still a remarkable woman."

Her eyes widened with shock.

"Shall we talk in the morning?" he asked.

She searched his features, needing to reassure herself that he wasn't playing word games with her.

She wanted to trust him. A part of her already did, she realized, although that little truth startled her right down to her bare toes. "In the morning," she confirmed.

"I need a home, Bailey."

He spoke so quietly that she whispered, "Is that all?"

A faint smile lifted the edges of his lips. "I need things I can't put into words yet."

"Why not?"

Patrick's smile faded. "The person I want to talk to can't hear me."

She glimpsed what resembled sadness in his eyes before he blinked it away. "I don't understand."

"I know, but that's all right." He turned away and walked to the open French doors. Pausing in the doorway, he glanced back at her. "Thank you, Bailey."

"For what?"

"For trying to trust me."

She watched him disappear into the shadow-darkened courtyard in the next heartbeat. Unable to stop herself, she went after him.

THREE

"Wait, please!"

Patrick paused and turned to look at Bailey as she hurried across the patio to catch up with him. She stumbled to a stop just a few feet in front of him.

Guided by pure instinct, he reached out to steady her. The urge to draw her into his arms was strong in the seconds that followed, but he quelled the impulse.

She stiffened, as though sensing his intent, then relaxed when he lowered his hands. "You seem . . . sad, and I don't understand why."

The breathless quality of her voice caused a visceral response deep inside his body. Patrick exhaled unevenly, then brought his hand up to caress her cheek gently. He stroked his fingertips across the silken surface, the warmth of her skin penetrating his fingertips and making them tingle. He reluctantly withdrew his hand and closed it into a tight fist. He couldn't afford to touch her again. She tempted him far more than she realized, and he sensed that he might not be able to restrain his hunger for her if he didn't stop now.

She frowned. "Patrick?"

"I'm not sad."

"Then what are you?"

"Don't you think I'm capable of feeling . . . regret for things that have happened or that might have been?"

The look she gave him conveyed her confusion. "You're a success, Patrick," Bailey reminded him.

"In some ways. In others, I've failed."

"Are you talking about Jeremy?"

"Not really."

Something in his expression prompted her admission, "You were right when you said that he made his own choices. I have no right to hold anyone else responsible for them."

"I'm glad to hear you say that. I have enough penance," he said, his choice of the word he'd used earlier in the day drawing a faint smile from her, "of my own to do without taking on anyone else's transgressions."

"No one is perfect," she offered thoughtfully, then studied him at length before speaking again. "Do you mind if I ask what else it is that you regret?"

One of the things he appreciated about the new Bailey was her directness, even if he didn't wish to pursue the list of regrets he'd compiled in recent years. He comforted himself with the mental reminder that he'd undertaken a major change in his life so that he would have fewer regrets to deal with in the future.

"I guess you do mind."

Patrick shrugged. "What I regret isn't important right now."

"Double-talk time?" she asked, her voice cool enough to leave a layer of frost on anything within a ten-foot radius.

He felt the chill. "Perhaps, perhaps not," he said, cautioning himself that if he made the mistake of revealing his longing for her all those years ago—and now—he would probably never see her again.

"There's no *perhaps* about it."

He exhaled, the sound heavy with the emotions he concealed for both their sakes. "Forgive me?"

"For what?" she questioned, sounding even more bewildered.

"For whatever it is you think I've done."

Looking baffled, she stared at him for a long moment.

He took her silence as a gift. He studied her face under the refracted light of the moon, drinking in the delicate contours of her features and the cascade of white-gold hair that tumbled across her shoulders and down her back. He felt as if he'd been given a reprieve of sorts, a chance to memorize her once more.

"Did you plan all this?" she finally asked.

He understood her meaning. "I didn't plan anything, Bailey. How could I have orchestrated our encounter this afternoon? I never knew your maiden name, so I couldn't have known that your company was handling the well drilling."

"You're a clever man."

Why deny the truth? his conscience prodded. "It goes with the territory. I won't apologize for who I am."

"I'm not asking you for an apology, but I don't like subterfuge, and I loathe it when anyone tries to manipulate me."

"I'm not a fool, Bailey."

"You have a reputation for being utterly relentless when you have a goal."

She knew him too well, he realized. He kept his tone mild. "That's not a crime."

"I didn't say it was."

He smiled. "But you're thinking it, aren't you?"

"Perhaps," she admitted.

"There's that word again, but thank you."

"For what? Being honest?"

"I've always appreciated that quality in you."

"It isn't considered an asset by some people."

"I will never be one of those people," he assured her.

"You implied that earlier. My head tells me you're right, but I'm having trouble separating you from what happened with Jeremy."

"Please try."

"I'm not sure I can. I meant it before when I said that people like you frighten me."

"Then I'll try not to frighten you."

"Easier said than done, I'm afraid."

"I know." It continued to amaze him that she didn't realize the extent of her power over him.

"I won't be managed, Patrick."

"I wouldn't do that to you." He'd tried to, though, during a crucial juncture in her ex-husband's career, and they both knew it, so he couldn't fault her caution.

"Why is my trust such an issue for you?"

"It just is, Bailey. It always has been."

"For all intents and purposes, we're strangers."

He smiled, but his expression was tinged with melancholy. "We've never been strangers, and you know that as well as I do."

"You're not making any sense," she countered, the edge returning to her voice.

He shrugged, but the gesture was anything but careless. Her defensiveness was back full force, and he knew he had to deal with it until he succeeded in dispelling it once and for all. "Not everything in life makes sense. It doesn't have to."

She released a gust of air. "You have a talent for talking in circles."

He massaged the back of his neck, then glanced at his watch. "Let's not pursue this, all right? You're tired, and I have another meeting tonight."

"Good night, then." Bailey turned on her heel and retraced her steps to the open French doors.

Patrick wanted to go after her, but he managed not to. He simply waited until she'd closed and secured the doors before walking the rest of his way to the limo waiting for him in the driveway.

As the limo driver guided the vehicle down the street for the short trip to the Biltmore Hotel in Montecito, he couldn't help thinking that Bailey Kincaid was no longer the innocent lamb who'd been led to emotional slaughter by his client. She'd fulfilled her promise, becoming the kind of woman who knew how to stand up for herself, those she cared about, and what she believed to be right. He knew she'd learned those particular lessons at great personal expense, just as he knew that he'd had a part, however peripherally, in teaching her them.

Patrick reached for the file on the seat beside him. Although he tried to concentrate on the material that Jeanne had prepared for him to read prior to his late-evening meeting, his thoughts refused to move beyond Bailey.

He closed the file and set it aside. He wondered, as he leaned his head back against the headrest and closed his eyes, if she even realized that she'd relaxed her stance with him and allowed her native compassion to shine through. He'd felt her concern for him, not just her frustration when he refused to be more specific in his responses to her questions. He told himself that it was possible that she would eventually abandon her mistrust of everything and everyone associated with the film industry, primarily because he didn't want to believe anything else.

Bailey forced herself out of bed when her alarm clock rang shortly before dawn the next morning. She always set it for at least an hour earlier than necessary. She liked easing into her day, not rushing into it full tilt the way Jeff did. He'd always accused her of needing time to contemplate her navel before she dealt with the world. The truth was that she enjoyed lingering over the morning newspaper while sipping a cup of coffee, then wandering out to the patio between her cottage and the main house, where she fussed over the roses planted during her childhood by her late father.

She felt close to Big Jake Kincaid when she cared for his roses. She missed her father more than ever on this particular morning. She missed the ever-present twinkle in his bright blue eyes, missed the way he'd cherished his family with a thousand and one thoughtful gestures, and missed his ability to listen when she wrestled with a problem, no matter how simple or complex.

It wasn't that her father had ever tried to solve her problems for her. Instead, he'd acted as a sounding board so that she learned to make solid decisions on her own.

As she fingered the delicate petals of a long-stemmed Mr. Lincoln rose, Bailey didn't have to wonder for very long about what Big Jake would have thought of Patrick Sutton, despite the latter's connection to Hollywood, and her father's disdain for the people who had almost destroyed his daughter's self-confidence.

She suspected that Big Jake and Patrick would have liked and respected each other, as much for their similarities as for their differences. Both strong-willed, both capable of taking on any challenge that came their way, they would have understood each other, she realized.

Sighing softly, she moved onto the next rosebush. Bailey didn't trust her own judgment where Patrick was concerned, but there was no one to talk to about him, no one to confide in about the emotions that flooded her every time she thought about him. In truth, she'd thought of him far too often during the last five years, and she'd always felt overwhelmed and unnerved whenever he'd strolled through her mind.

A car door suddenly slammed, drawing her attention. Expecting to see her brother, she glanced through the open design of the nearby wrought-iron gate. Her eyes widened when she saw Patrick Sutton as he leaned down to speak to the driver of his limo.

What in the world did he think he was doing? she wondered. Did he honestly believe that he could hound her into giving him what he wanted?

Patrick smiled as he approached the gate. "I remembered that you once said you were an early riser."

Bailey cautioned, "If you've come to pressure me again about fulfilling the drilling contract, don't waste your breath. In fact, if you say one word about water wells, I *will* cancel it."

She watched his smile widen as he unfastened the gate latch and strolled toward her. She was so annoyed by his presumption that he was welcome, she nearly pitched the watering can she held directly at his head.

Patrick glanced at her white-knuckled grip on the watering can. "I believe you." He raised the bakery box he held. "I've brought a peace offering from Antoine's."

"You're assuming I haven't had breakfast." Bailey heard her stomach gurgle as soon as the words left her mouth. She flushed.

"That sounded like a definite I-haven't-eaten-yet response to me."

"You also have a hell of a lot of nerve showing up here without a telephone call, but I guess I shouldn't be surprised."

"Guilty as charged, but I was hoping you'd be pleasantly surprised."

She glared at him while her heart tripped recklessly beneath her breasts. He looked too good to resist in his open-necked pinstripe shirt, black trousers, and deck shoes. Not a pretty man by any stretch of the imagination, he was big and solid. Adding insult to injury was the fact that his angular features displayed the force of his personality. He reminded her of a tornado, one capable of consuming anything in its path—including her, if she didn't watch herself.

His gaze dipped once more to the watering can. "Shall I also assume that you've managed to contain the violent impulse you just had?"

She freely confessed, "You are the only person who's ever inspired that particular impulse in me, but how did you know?"

"You get this look on your face when you've had enough. I noticed it yesterday, and it wasn't too hard to figure out what you were thinking." He smiled. "I wonder what a shrink would make of your reaction to me."

"We'll never know, since I don't need psychiatric care," she informed him, shocked that he'd read her so accurately at the drilling site. "What I need is some peace and quiet."

"This is a peace offering of sorts."

"Don't twist my words. You're not about to give me a dime's worth of peace until you get what you want."

"You know me well."

"I don't know if I want to know you at all." *Liar*, her conscience screeched. *Shut up!*

"If I thought that was true, Bailey, I wouldn't be here at all."

She swore under her breath, but something in his suddenly serious tone made her believe what he'd just said. She wondered then if he suspected the emotional conflict he'd always caused her. She hoped not, but she vowed then and there to be on her guard.

His grin widened as he strolled past her and made his way to the table and chairs in the center of the patio. By the time he'd placed the pastry box in the middle of the glass tabletop, he'd managed to straighten out his face. "Got any coffee left?"

Bailey shoved the gate. It clanged as it slammed shut. After depositing the watering can on a nearby bench, she said a quick prayer that Jeff had already gone to work. If he tripped over Patrick Sutton at this hour of the morning, he'd grill him like a felony suspect.

She wasn't actually afraid that Patrick would be intimidated by her brother. She didn't think that anything or anyone could really intimidate him. What she didn't want to witness was Jeff doing his brotherly duty. The very idea of that kind of behavior on his part gave her hives.

Bailey crossed the patio, suddenly conscious that all she was wearing was an ankle-length nightshirt. She felt exposed, and too vulnerable for words. "This is not a good idea," she informed him.

"Could we discuss it over breakfast?"

She scowled at him. "You're impossible."

"That's what I've heard," he confessed. He popped the lid on the box and tipped it toward her for her inspection as she approached the patio table.

Her gaze fell to the contents of the box, an almond-studded confection topped with a transparent sugar glaze, and her stomach promptly gurgled again with appreciation. "Very nice, but I wasn't expecting company."

"One cup of coffee, then I'll leave," he pledged.

"One cup," she repeated.

"And a slice of coffee cake?"

Bailey hesitated, all the while hating her weak-kneed response to him. She didn't want him to leave, but she didn't want him to stay, either. Blast the man! she thought, certain she would in fact be dealing with some serious mental-health issues if he didn't depart Santa Barbara in the next twenty-four hours.

"Earth to Bailey."

She snapped back to the present, "One slice," she grudgingly said, trusting the instinct to be very specific about her terms. "But then you're on your way. Agreed?"

"Of course."

She frowned at him, suspicion joining the heat surging through her senses. "That was too easy."

Patrick chuckled, his dark eyes so filled with pleasure that she heard an alarm bell go off in her head. He's up to something, she decided, her frown persisting as she watched him.

He lifted his hands like a man with a gun trained on him. "I didn't come here to harass you, I promise. I simply wanted to share breakfast with a beautiful woman."

Bailey shook her head, not bothering to conceal

her disbelief. "I'm not buying islands or bridges this morning."

She heard his laughter as she marched across the patio with as much dignity as she could muster while attired in a shapeless nightshirt from her college days.

Once she entered her cottage, Bailey located her bathrobe, slipped into it, and belted it snugly, then made her way to the kitchen. She hurriedly poured the contents of the coffeepot into a carafe. After tucking several paper napkins into her pocket, she retrieved two mugs from the kitchen counter.

A little voice in her head suggested that plates and utensils might not be an altogether bad idea, but she ignored the mental nudge to be a proper hostess. She'd run out of hands and this wasn't a planned meal, so her hospitality had definite limits as far as she was concerned.

Squaring her shoulders, she rejoined Patrick on the patio. Bailey told herself that she could and would handle his intrusion into her morning. She counseled herself to be very, very careful with him. Sparring verbally with Patrick Sutton was a no-win proposition, so she resolved not even to try a tactic like that on the legendary negotiator for Hollywood's elite.

Just being near him seduced her senses and her emotions. The scent of his aftershave had already knocked her for a loop, and her awareness of his well-muscled anatomy had her imagination doing cartwheels. Since calming down didn't seem to be an option, she settled for the appearance of composure. Bailey placed the carafe, mugs, and napkins on the table and then sat down in the chair positioned opposite Patrick.

"Please help yourself," she invited.

Patrick accepted her invitation, filled both mugs with coffee, then claimed one for himself and sank back in his chair. "I think I envy you."

"Why?" She leaned forward and reached for the remaining mug as she waited for his reply. When she felt the tremors moving through her fingers, she gripped her mug even more tightly with both hands.

"This is a great way to start the day." He glanced around the patio, his appreciation for the lush garden-style patio apparent.

"I make a habit of it every morning." She took a sip of the steaming brew, then placed her mug on the table for safety's sake. "Considering the location of your building site, you'll have a panoramic view of the Pacific all the way to the horizon."

"This seems more"—he paused for a moment—"intimate, somehow."

"The plants have been here for a long time," she remarked neutrally.

Patrick's smile was a little lazy and a lot seductive as he peered at her. "I honestly wasn't thinking of the foliage."

Bailey tensed inside as his voice started to weave a spell around her. "I assume you have a real reason for being here."

He chuckled. "You probably won't believe me."

"Try me," she urged.

"I woke up thinking about you this morning."

Another woman might have read more into his remark or even been flattered, but she prided herself on not being a fool. Patrick had to have a motive, and she felt confident that she understood it. "I told you I'd call you when I made a decision," she reminded him.

"I thought we weren't going to talk about the well drilling."

"It's our only link, Patrick, so I guess we'd better talk about it."

"Do you remember my son?" he asked, changing the subject without warning.

Although startled by his question, Bailey recovered quickly. "Daniel? Of course, I remember him."

"It turns out that you were a major influence in his life."

"I was his tutor for all of three months when he was in high school, so I doubt that I had much influence over him." She smiled, remembering the gangly teen with an oddly mature sense of the ridiculous.

"He's a geology major at UC Santa Barbara," Patrick said with quiet pride. "He's doing very well. Dean's list all the way. He graduates next year."

"I'm surprised by his choice of study, but I'm not at all surprised by his grades. He was a wonderful student when we worked together." Falling silent, Bailey grappled with her shock. She remembered Daniel as a bright but somewhat unmotivated student. After meeting him at a party for the Sutton Group clients, she'd offered to tutor him while he prepared for his SATs.

She'd liked Daniel's dry humor and irreverent perspective on his father's clients. She'd also felt comfortable with him at a time in her life when she was struggling to come to terms with a failing marriage. Daniel had allowed her to indulge her passion for teaching, and she knew she would always remember him with great affection.

"You were an excellent teacher, Bailey."

"Tutor. I never got certified."

"But you intend to, don't you?"

"Someday, perhaps."

Patrick frowned.

"Now, what?" she asked, sounding more prickly than she intended.

"Dreams shouldn't be abandoned, Bailey. They feed the soul."

"I agree, but sometimes they have to be deferred for a while."

"Daniel still talks about you."

She smiled. "Will you tell him hello for me the next time you speak with him?"

"Of course I will. I'm having lunch with him today. Do you mind if I let him know how to reach you?"

Bailey hesitated, torn between wanting to see Daniel again and concerned that any interest in him from her quarter might prompt Patrick to think that he could wander in and out of her life at will.

"He's a polite kid, Bailey, and he won't impose on you. I also won't draw any inappropriate conclusions if you express an interest in my son."

She searched his features, and she saw a look that she'd always seen in her own father's face when he spent time with his children. Profound love. The kind of unconditional love that every child deserves. The kind of love that Patrick had always displayed for his son. "It must have been tough raising him alone."

"Like riding a roller coaster most of the time, but we both survived the process. After Rebecca died, Daniel gave me the emotional focus to resume my life. He's the reason I survived the grief."

She shifted uneasily in her chair, not certain she wanted him to confide in her. Honesty forced her to admit to herself that it made him more human, as well as vulnerable in ways that she'd never associated with him.

She knew that Patrick had been a good father, despite his mover-and-shaker lifestyle. She'd seen evidence of that fact during her tutoring sessions with Daniel. It had been clear to her that Patrick's son was emotionally secure, even if he'd felt constrained by a school system that failed to challenge his intellect.

"Am I making you uncomfortable?" Patrick asked.

Bailey shook her head, although tendrils of regret had begun to twine about her heart. She longed for children, but life hadn't been generous in that department. Not yet, anyway. She knew she'd been better off not having children, given her divorced state. "You can give Daniel my phone number, if he asks for it."

"He'll ask. He never had a chance to say goodbye before you left Los Angeles."

She remembered how bad she'd felt after she penned a letter saying farewell to the then seventeen-year-old boy. She'd deliberately omitted a return address, preferring to sever all of her ties at the time. "I'd like to see him again."

"You aren't alone in the losses you've suffered, Bailey."

She nodded her agreement. People died. People divorced. And other people simply survived. Bailey wanted more from life, though, than survival. She wanted a real partner. A man with his own success, a sense of humor, and the ability to embrace a shared sense of purpose. She also wanted the passion and intensity of an enduring love. Her parents had had that kind of a relationship, so she knew it was possible. For now, she let herself hope that it would be possible for her someday.

"You once told me you wanted a houseful of children. Still feel that way?" he asked.

Bailey took a steadying breath, then answered his question with two of her own. "Why are we talking about children, Patrick? What does this conversation have to do with your current agenda?"

The image of innocence, he said, "I'm just curious."

She shook her head. "You're never just curious."

"You know me too well."

"I know what ambitious people are like. The world's full of them."

"That's how things get accomplished," he reminded her in a deceptively mild-sounding tone of voice.

She spoke quietly. "It's also how people get trampled in the name of some higher purpose."

Patrick straightened in his chair and set aside his coffee mug. "I'm not the enemy."

"So you keep telling me, but I'm not altogether sure what you are or what it is you're trying to accomplish. And until I know, I will reserve the right to be suspicious of you."

Patrick slid back his chair and got to his feet. He circled the glass-topped table. He didn't rush. He moved, instead, in that gracefully predatory way of his that revealed his physical prowess as a man.

Bailey surged to her feet before he reached her. She gripped the back of the wrought-iron chair she'd just abandoned, aware that it wasn't much of a barrier against anyone. Especially Patrick. Still, she held her ground, feeling vaguely foolish and thoroughly disconcerted.

"Relax, Bailey."

How? she wondered, her inner tension mounting. *How do I relax with you close enough to reach out and touch?* She tightened her hold on the chair, willing herself to stay in control, willing herself not to hurl herself at him.

His gaze fell to her white knuckles. He gave her a look of helplessness that she'd never seen in his features before, and it startled her. He said nothing as he simply looked at her.

Bailey felt her own confusion and anxiety tangle up inside her. "I'm sorry," she finally whispered. "I'm acting as if I've lost my mind."

"I'm the one who's sorry."

"Don't apologize. It makes me feel even more like an adolescent."

"Do I frighten you that much?" he asked.

She shook her head, realizing that she feared herself and what she wanted to experience with him.

"Tell me what's wrong, and I'll do everything in my power to fix it."

She laughed. She couldn't help herself. Was there an inoculation that would make her immune to Patrick Sutton? She seriously doubted it. Medical science wasn't that advanced yet.

He looked a little shocked by her laughter. And even more confused. "Why don't you sit down? You look like you're about to fall on your nose."

"I'm fine." She reclaimed her dignity and her

sanity by the sheer force of her will. "This is the craziest situation I've ever been in."

"I thought I was the crazy one."

"We're both crazy," she announced, noticing that his expression gentled in the seconds that followed.

"You may be right."

"We need a truce, you and I."

"I'm listening."

"I don't like to fail, and cowardice doesn't suit me," she said, using his words from their meeting the night before.

He half smiled. "Ditto."

"And I really resent having my jobs disrupted by unknown vandals."

Patrick nodded. "Makes total sense to me."

She smiled for the first time that day. "I thought it might."

"Tell me more," he encouraged.

"I'm proposing a trial of sorts. Once the equipment we need arrives from Oklahoma, we'll get back to work. My foreman and his helpers will stay on the job as long as there aren't any further acts of vandalism. If there are any other problems, then I'll have to pull my people, and I won't offer a refund on the project even if we don't complete the job. That's as fair as I know how to be."

"You're being more than fair, but there's one more thing I'd like to add to your proposal."

"And that is?"

"A security guard. I'll cover the expenses involved."

She liked the idea, even though it bothered her that this was the first time in the history of Kincaid Drilling that such a thing had been necessary. "I'll speak to Jeff."

"Your brother?"

She nodded. "He's in law enforcement."

Patrick extended his hand. "Then we have an understanding."

Bailey accepted his handshake, a frisson of awareness stealing into her mind the instant their palms met. She inhaled sharply, but she didn't jerk free of Patrick. Instead, she met his gaze, and the desire she saw in his eyes made her respiration choppy.

He shifted her chair aside with his free hand without breaking their connection, then gently drew her forward. "Thank you."

"You're welcome." She heard herself say the words as she stared up at him, aware even as she spoke that she was in danger of drowning in the dark depths of his thickly lashed eyes.

"I feel that way now," he said, his tone low and intimate.

"The situation might fall apart," she cautioned, her gaze still locked on his face.

"We can deal with it. Together." He tugged her even closer.

Bailey didn't resist. She sensed that she couldn't

have even if she'd wanted to, although she had the presence of mind to ask, "What are you doing?"

He curved his hands over her shoulders. "I want to hold you, but only if you want the same thing." He waited then, waited for her to chart the course ahead.

Unable to resist the instincts that guided her, she stepped forward and found herself almost overwhelmed by the heat emanating from his sturdy body. She felt as though she'd stepped off a precipice and into midair, free-falling into a depthless canyon of glittering sensory awareness that astounded her.

As Patrick brought his arms around her and simply held her, Bailey heard a heavy sigh escape him. She felt the shudder that moved through him a few seconds later, then the not-so-subtle tightening of his powerful body.

She inhaled and exhaled shakily, and it suddenly occurred to her that Patrick Sutton was far more than a skilled power broker. What made him unique also placed him in a position of isolation, setting him apart from the world at large and people in general. But his isolation hadn't eliminated more human responses like sensitivity, vulnerability, or even simple need.

He was, she realized, a man who was human enough to want tenderness and affection. A man who'd struggled with grief and overcome it. A man who'd raised his son with love. A man who'd triumphed in a community founded on half-truths and illusion. And a man who seemed to want her with the same intensity that she wanted him.

Bailey trembled, her shock moving through her in waves and crashing against her emotional resistance to him like an angry surf. She felt the tightening of his encircling arms when she sagged against him. He kept her upright as her desire for him began to eclipse her fear. She realized at that moment that she couldn't have moved away from him for all the riches in the world. She lacked the strength and the will.

As she grappled with her hunger for him she slowly slid her arms around his waist and rested her forehead against his chest.

"I've missed you, Bailey Kincaid."

Shock and amazement slammed together inside her. Lifting her head, she peered up at him, but the moment shattered when a voice she didn't recognize sounded from the edge of the patio.

"Sir, you have an urgent phone call."

Patrick cursed, but he didn't release her. Bailey repeated the word he'd just muttered in the privacy of her mind.

"He wouldn't have disturbed us if it weren't important," he said, his voice rich with regret.

She nodded, too dazed to do much else.

Patrick stepped away from her and crossed the patio. Bailey sank into her chair, watching as he accepted the cellular phone from his limo driver. The look of shock on his face jarred her, and she knew then that something was terribly wrong. Her first thought was of his son.

Patrick finished his call, then retraced his steps across the patio. "Tommy Dunlap's been in a serious car accident. The doctors don't think he'll survive."

Bailey gave him a blank look. It took her a moment to make the connection. "The documentary film director?"

"Yes," he confirmed.

Bailey surged up from her chair. Driven by the instinct to comfort, she approached Patrick. "I'm very sorry."

"So am I."

"Is there anything I can do?"

"Not really, but I appreciate the sentiment. I need to get back to Los Angeles."

Bailey walked with him to the wrought-iron gate, uncertain of what to say to Patrick when they paused and faced each other.

"I'll be back in a few days," he said, his expression bleak.

"All right." She reached out and placed her hand over his heart. She felt the steadiness of the beat beneath her fingertips. "Don't neglect yourself, Patrick. It's easy to do that kind of thing when tragedies occur."

He stroked her cheek, sadness reflected in the brief smile he gave her, and then he was gone. Bailey watched the limo glide down the street until it disappeared from sight.

As she walked into her cottage she struggled to make sense of what had just happened between herself and Patrick. Bailey struggled, as well, with the painful reminder of just how fleeting life and happiness could be.

FOUR

Bailey devoted herself exclusively to work in the days that followed. It was necessary given the number of water-well drilling jobs under way, not simply because she didn't want to dwell on the longing she felt for Patrick. He never left her thoughts, however, and she grew anxious about his ability to dominate her every waking moment. She'd lowered her guard with him during his early morning visit, and she repeatedly questioned her own behavior.

She kept reminding herself that Patrick Sutton symbolized everything she mistrusted, and she clung to that reminder in the same way that a drowning victim clung to a life preserver. The fact that he made no effort to contact her, justified or not, strengthened Bailey's resolve to treat him like any other client once he returned to Santa Barbara.

She also discounted her desire for him as nothing more than a skillful man's ability to make her feel vulnerable and needy. She slept fitfully each night, however, her dreams almost too sensual to bear. She even lost her temper with her employees more often than she had in the four years since taking over the running of the company following Big Jake's death. Her conscience informed her that she was being unfair to Patrick, not just the people who worked for her. She ignored the screechy little voice as best she could. All she needed was a good night's sleep.

The replacement pipe and equipment needed to resume drilling at Fox Ridge arrived several days late, courtesy of a computer glitch at the order desk of their Oklahoma supplier.

While Pete Higgins and his helpers began reassembling the drilling tower a week to the day following the third act of vandalism at the site, Bailey sat at her desk in her office. She absently munched on an apple, her sole concession to the necessity of eating lunch that day, as she studied the final draft of a hydro-geologic survey for a prospective client, which was spread out in front of her.

The phone rang, but she tuned out the sound at first. When she remembered that her secretary was running errands during her lunch hour, she grabbed it on the fifth ring. The voice Bailey heard on the other end of the line set off alarm bells in her head an instant later.

"I just got back into town."

Patrick! Bailey scrambled for the emotional balance she'd vowed to maintain with him upon his return to Santa Barbara. She said nothing, as a result, although she gripped the phone so tightly that her hand started to ache. She took a shallow breath, and then told herself to settle down.

"Bailey?"

"I'm here. What can I do for you, Patrick?" Great, she thought, wondering why in the world she'd asked him such a leading question.

He chuckled.

The low sound of his laughter swept over her like a flash fire. Unwilling to be incinerated, body and soul, by this man, she willed herself to stay strong.

"You can have dinner with me tonight, Bailey Kincaid. We'll celebrate."

"I don't think—" she began.

He broke in, "Tommy came out of his coma last night. The doctors tell me the odds are good that he'll make a full recovery."

She softened, despite her resolve not to be swayed by him under any circumstances. "I'm glad for you, and for your friend."

"So, what do you say? Feel like celebrating with me and bringing me up to speed on the work at Fox Ridge at the same time?"

"I take it that Charlie Cannon hasn't spoken to you," she said, not really able to begrudge him his buoyant mood.

"Charlie's away on business for the rest of the week, but I took a quick look at the building site on my way into town. Pete Higgins and his crew were unloading replacement pipe."

"Did you speak with Pete?"

"I didn't want to interrupt him. Shall I pick you up or meet you somewhere?"

She hedged yet again, but she could feel her resistance to him crumbling with every passing second. "I'm shoulder-deep in work right now."

"You have to eat, Bailey." He paused. "It's been a tough week, and I'd really like to see you."

The gentleness of his voice caught her off guard, as did his admission that almost losing a friend had been hard on him. She wanted to see Patrick, almost as much as she felt compelled to fight the attraction that existed between them. The chance to spend time with him won out, however, and even as she called herself a very foolish woman, she surrendered to the inevitable.

"How about Michaelina's at the pier?" he asked. "You set the time, and I'll have Jeanne arrange my schedule around you."

Bailey expected she'd regret this little venture into the world of self-torture. In the meantime, though, she would have dinner with Patrick, if for no other reason than to remind herself that he endangered her emotions and the peace of mind she'd fought so hard to attain.

"My ego's in danger of being bruised if you don't say yes," he teased.

"All right, Patrick." She glanced at her appointment calendar. "I can meet you at seven."

"Good. I've missed you." With that parting comment, he severed the connection.

Bailey slowly replaced the receiver in the phone's cradle. He'd missed her? Why did he insist on saying things like that to her? she wondered. As she sank back in her chair she clasped her shaking hands together in her lap and let out the breath trapped in her lungs.

The feeling that she should never have agreed to meet Patrick for dinner intensified as the rest of her day unfolded. By the time she parked her Jeep in the public lot at the pier that evening, Bailey's nerves were strung tightly enough to snap under the slightest pressure.

The hostess of the restaurant guided her to the table. Patrick stood, a smile on his face that failed to conceal the fatigue shadowing his eyes. He drew out her chair for her, then took his own.

"Welcome," he said once they were alone.

"Thank you."

Bailey scanned his features with what she suspected was the all-too-obvious hunger of a woman starved for the sight of the man she deeply desired. She couldn't help wondering when he'd last had a solid night of sleep. It bothered her more than she cared to admit that she felt concerned about his welfare.

Needing something to do with her hands, she reached for her napkin and placed it in her lap. "You look exhausted." The words slipped out before she could stop them.

Patrick shrugged. "I am, but it couldn't be helped. Tommy's parents flew in from Minneapolis the morning after the accident. They weren't at all prepared for the touch-and-go nature of his condition. I couldn't leave them to fend for themselves."

"So you maintained a weeklong vigil at the hospital with them?" she speculated quietly.

"After a fashion. I commandeered the office of a vacationing doctor and worked from the hospital while I kept a close watch on them. They're good people, and they were pretty overwhelmed at the prospect of losing their only child."

"That was very generous of you."

Had he been a man with a conscience during her marriage to Jeremy? she suddenly wondered as she studied him. She'd always believed that he, and people like him, lacked that particular attribute, but then perhaps she hadn't wanted to see it. She felt a stab of guilt at the possibility that she might have been so blind to everything and everyone around her.

He smiled as he reached for his wineglass. "Tommy might be an obsessive pain in the butt when it comes to his documentaries, but he's been a friend for a long time."

She pondered his comment while she tasted her wine. "And you don't abandon your friends?"

His humor faded, and he answered her in a serious tone of voice. "I try very hard not to, Bailey, even if I don't always succeed."

She nodded as she put down her wineglass and

sank back in her chair. She shifted her gaze beyond Patrick to the picture-postcard ambience of the natural bay that edged up against the community of Santa Barbara.

Anchored sailboats bobbed on the gentle waves while several small motorized crafts, their running lights glowing in the encroaching dusk, eased across the water. The open windows of the restaurant allowed her to enjoy the balmy, salt-laden breezes drifting in off the Pacific.

"What are you thinking right now?" he asked.

Bailey found the courage to voice her thoughts. "I'm wondering why we're having dinner together. We could have confined ourselves to a phone conversation."

"You're not buying the idea of a celebration?"

"No," she whispered. "I don't know Tommy Dunlap. I wish him a full recovery, of course, but I don't have a thing to do with him or his life."

"You have something to do with my life."

"Only in a very peripheral sense."

"That's where you're wrong, Bailey. In fact, you couldn't be more wrong."

"Don't play head games with me, Patrick. Please. I've never understood the rules, and I quite honestly have no desire to learn them."

"That's one of the things I've always appreciated about you. But then, I've always appreciated you, even when I had no right to."

She held up a hand, but she kept her voice low

as she insisted, "Stop right there, Patrick. I don't like revisiting the past."

"Why not?" he challenged, an unexpectedly sharp edge in his voice. "It's where you're living emotionally."

She reached for her purse and started to get up from the table, but something in Patrick's facial expression—sadness, perhaps—prompted her to sink back down in her chair.

"Life isn't simple or easy, so why should you be let off the hook while the rest of us mere mortals have to face the good and the bad? Why should you be exempt?" he asked.

"You think I'm a coward, don't you?"

"What I think would surprise the hell out of you. It would also send you running for cover. I'm trying, without getting a damn bit of credit for my efforts, not to overwhelm you."

She stiffened. "Do not swear at me."

"I'm not swearing at anyone, and you know it. Look, I feel as if I'm navigating a minefield. I also don't feel free to speak candidly to you. At least, not yet."

"I have a hard time believing that you're re-straining yourself," she shot back. "That's hardly your style."

"How can I safely do anything else? You're so gun-shy—thanks to Jeremy—that you instinctively think the worst of everyone. Especially me. As for my style, you have a lot left to learn about me before you make that kind of blanket judgment."

"You're wrong," Bailey protested, even though her conscience assured her that he wasn't at all wrong.

"Am I? I think we both know I'm right on target. What happens if I admit that I've thought about you more often during the last five years than any sane man should ever think about a woman who loathes the sight of him and what he represents?"

Shocked by his question, she didn't know what to say.

"I'm not supposed to tell you that I wanted you when you were married to Jeremy, am I? I'm very sure that you don't want to know that I felt as guilty as all hell about the feelings I had for you in those days, nor are you willing to acknowledge the fact that I kept my feelings and my hands to myself out of respect for you, Bailey. And, of course, I shouldn't think of admitting that the desire I feel for you is a far cry from anything I've ever felt for another woman. If I did, then you'd have to address some of the emotions you're feeling, wouldn't you?"

Bailey stared at him, still unable to speak as shock crashed around inside her like a wrecking ball. She'd never had even the slightest hint that Patrick wanted her. He'd always been polite to her, but she remembered him more as an aloof man who routinely juggled high-priced film stars and their egos.

"And I certainly can't risk telling you that I'm

worried about you, even though I see years of lone-liness ahead for you. I can't believe how afraid you are of any real emotions, aside from the ones you can control." He cursed, the word a coarse punctu-ation mark on his comments so far.

She released a shaken breath. "I don't loathe you, Patrick. I'll admit that there was a time when I was furious with what I perceived as your lack of moral standards."

He leaned closer and covered one of her hands with his own. "What do you feel now?"

Confusion. Terror. Shock. Desire so intense that it was about to cripple her common sense. Pick one. No, she thought, taking a mental left turn, pick them all, since they all apply. She tugged her hand free, but the heat of his touch lingered and blazed a path directly to her heart. "I'm not pre-pared to answer your question."

"You won't answer it. There's a difference."

"You're not being fair," she insisted in her own defense.

"Life isn't fair. Life's a whole basketload of things, and fair is rarely one of them."

"You sound . . ." She paused, her emotions raw as she grappled with her hunger for him, de-spite his stinging criticisms of a few moments ear-lier.

"Cynical?" he said, supplying the word for her. "I probably am, to a certain degree, but I'm also frustrated."

She seized the ball he'd just tossed at her and

ran with it, but she felt like an idiot as soon as she asked, "Is this about sex?"

"Don't, Bailey, don't you dare try to reduce our situation to that level. It insults us both, and I resent it."

"We do not have a *situation*."

He arched a thick dark brow. "What would you call it, then?"

She saw the control he exerted over himself as he sat very still and waited for her to supply an answer, all the while gripping the stem of his wineglass. Bailey feared he'd snap it and cut himself. Reaching out, she gently pushed his fingers away from the fragile crystal. Her caring gesture brought a baffled look to his face that tore at her heart.

Withdrawing her hands, she tucked them in her lap. In the moments that followed she accepted the fact that she was denying the obvious, so she decided to stop acting like a coward and a fool. Whatever the end result, she felt compelled to be honest. "I want you, Patrick Sutton, but you scare me absolutely witless most of the time. As for the future, I certainly don't intend to spend it alone. Does that about cover it, or are there any other issues that we need to get out in the open before we order our meals?" she asked with a calm that belied the emotional confusion she felt.

He shook his head, surprise and disbelief etched into his features. "When I think I know what you're going to say, you take one of your verbal left turns. You do realize, I hope, that you're the only woman I've ever known who makes me feel like an inexperienced adolescent."

"I seriously doubt that."

"You shouldn't doubt it at all. It's the truth."

"Why?" she asked, convinced now that he wanted more than sex from her. Was she even capable of having a relationship with a man like Patrick Sutton? she wondered. Or had she locked up her heart and thrown away the key in order to avoid all risks with any member of the opposite sex?

His exasperation resurfacing, he asked, "Do I have to have a reason for everything?"

"In my experience, most people do."

"Menus, sir?"

Bailey nearly jumped out of her skin. Patrick's sensually shaped mouth thinned to a rigid line.

She glanced at the waiter, who looked at her expectantly.

Patrick didn't bother to look at him at all. He simply commanded, "Leave them."

"Yes, sir." The waiter stepped backward two paces after depositing the menus at his elbow.

Bailey pretended he wasn't there. "I'm starved," she announced, grateful for the chance to regather her wits.

"So am I," Patrick admitted, sounding calmer. "Does that mean you're staying?"

It was her turn to smile. "You invited me for dinner, and I accepted, so you're obligated to feed me."

He shook his head, his sudden grin boyish

enough to ease the hard angles of his face. Reaching across the table, he took Bailey's hand, brought it to his lips, and pressed a kiss into her open palm.

"You shouldn't . . ."

"I should and you know it," he countered, "but I don't want to rush you."

He released her hand and met her gaze, the pleasure and laughter lighting up his eyes so inviting that Bailey felt faint. She exhaled shallowly.

She silently hoped he meant his comment about not rushing her, especially since she felt on the verge of total capitulation to her desire for him. She knew then that her heart was also in grave jeopardy, and she needed time to come to terms with that undeniable reality. She also needed time to figure out how to protect her emotions if she decided to get involved with Patrick.

"Talk to me," he ordered a few moments later, but the seductive undertone of his voice took the sting out of his command.

Bailey felt thoroughly seduced by him and by his voice. She was also very hungry, so she addressed the safer of the two subjects. "Lobster bisque, sliced tomatoes in balsamic vinegar and fresh herbs, grilled swordfish with rice, and sorbet for dessert."

Patrick grinned his approval. The waiter, still hovering within earshot, jotted down her order.

"Times two," Patrick said as he handed the waiter their menus. He then requested a bottle of

Chenin Blanc without ever taking his eyes off the woman seated opposite him.

"It's your turn to talk to me," she informed him.

He responded without hesitation. "I'm glad you decided to stay for dinner."

Feeling unexpectedly shy, Bailey studied him and saw nothing other than sincerity in his gaze as he looked back at her. She felt reassured enough to admit the truth. "I am too."

What she knew could have turned into a very strained meal for both of them became, instead, a chance for Bailey to learn more about Patrick's life. She consciously opened her mind and her senses to him, asking him questions about his past.

She discovered that he'd been an officer in the navy following his graduation from Harvard, much to the chagrin of both his parents and his economics professors. He even provided her with a few highlights of his tour of duty as a SEAL team leader, although he declined to get into any of the specifics of the work he'd done for the navy.

Bailey saw the wisdom of not pressing him, so she asked him questions about Daniel's childhood. He regaled her with stories about his son's early years, including excursions to Disneyland, camping trips, and coping with illnesses like chicken pox while dealing simultaneously with what was then a fledgling entertainment agency.

They talked about his hope that he'd guided Daniel in such a way that the boy had learned to balance goal setting with the need to maintain strong personal relationships. Bailey felt confident that Patrick has succeeded, even though she hadn't seen Daniel in several years.

Without any prodding at all, Patrick spoke at length about Rebecca, his late wife and Daniel's mother. He shared with her many of his memories of their three-year marriage—the challenge of starting a new business, the laughter, the joy. Although he admitted that her sudden death during the days after childbirth had almost reduced him to emotional rubble, Bailey saw evidence of his inner strength and courage. She also applauded his ability to transform his grief into a genuine devotion to his son.

His willingness to travel down memory lane for her added dimension and depth to Bailey's perception of Patrick as a man. She could no longer write him off as someone who lacked substance or integrity as a human being, and it served to remind her that he wouldn't ever be just a client.

He was quite remarkable in a variety of ways, and she knew she couldn't pretend otherwise ever again. That her hunger for him intensified as he opened up didn't surprise her, although it still worried her. Placing her heart at risk wasn't something she'd willingly done since Jeremy, but she felt on the brink of taking such a risk.

"Why didn't you ever remarry?" she asked once they finished their after-dinner coffee and sorbet.

She knew her question was bold, but she felt compelled to ask it.

"I've asked myself that question many times over the years," he admitted. "At first I told myself that Daniel needed all of my attention, but the truth was a little harsher. I didn't want to risk losing someone I loved, so I avoided the possibility of commitment altogether."

She understood how painful that kind of self-honesty could be. She still grappled with the issue of betrayal. "It must have been difficult to be that honest with yourself."

"Not really, although it took me several years to realize what I was doing." Patrick shrugged. "I immersed myself in my son's needs and in my work. The bottom line is that I finally faced what I was doing to myself."

"And then what?" Bailey asked as she set aside her napkin.

"I started dating." He tilted his head to the side. "Are you sure you want to hear this? Talking about the women I've seen socially isn't exactly how I envisioned our time together."

"Please go on." She might not like the idea of imagining him with other women, but how could she begrudge him a normal life?

"I've had three relationships, all fairly long-term, since Becca's death."

She didn't ask the question she wanted to ask when he paused again, but she was curious, nonetheless. Why hadn't he married?

"Every time I thought about marriage, I held back."

"Why?"

"Probably for the same reason you haven't made a commitment, Bailey. I wanted something more than what was there, even though I couldn't exactly define what that more was."

His candor unsettled her, even though she understood what he meant. She said nothing. What could she say without revealing her own dreams and longings?

"And then, to make a long story a lot less boring, I decided to make some major changes in my life."

"I don't think you're boring, Patrick."

Their waiter materialized in the next instant in order to return Patrick's credit card. When he asked if they wanted anything else, both Bailey and Patrick declined, and the young man moved on to the diners at a nearby table.

"You feel more relaxed now, don't you?"

She laughed as she inclined her head in agreement. "I'm also definitely well fed," she confessed as she reached for her purse. "I think I ate too much."

"You look perfect to me," he said as they got up from the table.

"Thank you."

"You're more than welcome." Patrick guided her through the crowded restaurant. Once they stepped outside, he took her free hand. "I'm not ready to let you go. How about a walk along the pier?"

The warmth of his touch sent a flush through her body. "No meetings to rush off to?"

"Not a one," he assured her.

"I'd love a walk, then."

"You can run an extra mile tomorrow." He grinned when she flashed a surprised glance at him.

Bailey paused once they reached the railing of the pier. "How did you know I'm a runner?"

"Your legs."

"My legs?"

"The muscle tone. Despite your notable curves, you've got the lean, toned body of a marathoner."

She'd taken up running as a way to counteract the stress of work. It had become an important part of her daily life, a time to reflect on both personal and professional issues. She'd discovered that, along the way, it helped take the edge off the absence of physical intimacy in her life, even though running hadn't ever eliminated her desire for a healthy physical relationship with the right man.

"You're very observant, Patrick."

"Where you're concerned, I am," he admitted. "And I definitely approve of the new you, by the way."

She smiled at him as they resumed their stroll. "Thank you again."

"Just pointing out the obvious."

"You mentioned making changes in your life. Is Santa Barbara part of a larger plan?"

"Very much so. I never intended to remain in Los Angeles."

"Ah, the land of smoke and mirrors."

"It's more than that, of course, but the lifestyle can wear a person down after a while."

"I know, Patrick. Believe me, I know."

"Unlike you, though, I'll never condemn the entire community. There are a lot of good people in that town, but there are a lot of users, as well."

"I can't be objective about it," she confessed, "especially since I always seemed to err on the side of bad judgment when I opened myself up to people."

"Maybe you expected too much of yourself in those days," he speculated. "You were very young and newly married. You had a lot to deal with."

"Was I that obvious?" she asked.

"You were that earnest."

She exhaled softly, somewhat taken aback by his insightfulness. When she glanced at him, she saw compassion and warmth in his gaze. "In the final analysis, I did expect too much of myself. I was convinced that I could be the perfect geologist and the perfect wife. I was wrong, though."

"And so you decided that you were a failure?"

She gave him a sad look. "I felt like one."

"You're a harsh judge of yourself."

"I faced my mistakes, Patrick. I took responsibility for them."

"But you forgot to forgive yourself along the

way, so maybe you should try doing that now," he suggested.

"I thought I had," she said.

He shook his head. "I don't mean for the errors you think you made. We all make mistakes. I've certainly made my share. Jeremy, too, for that matter. I'm talking about forgiving yourself for being human."

"I've tried."

"Perhaps you should keep trying," he urged quietly.

"I'm making every effort not to live in the past, but those years taught me lessons I don't think I can unlearn."

"Perhaps you won't need them in the future. Perhaps your life will take a whole new turn," he said speculatively.

She seriously doubted it, but she let it go. What was the point?

Patrick fell silent then, too, and peered up at the moon. A perfectly shaped sphere, it glowed with the brightness of a brilliant morning sun.

As she stood beside Patrick at the railing Bailey studied his profile. She sensed his disappointment in her. Although it bothered her, she refused to defend herself. She knew her caution was justified. She wanted nothing whatsoever to do with his world, and she couldn't imagine ever feeling otherwise.

Bailey shifted her footing and turned to glance around. Couples of all ages, some holding hands, others chatting and laughing, strolled along the pier. They all reminded her of the isolation she'd endured since her divorce. She recalled the difficulty of adjusting to life as a single woman. She liked her life now, liked the independence she had and the sense of accomplishment she derived from her work.

She knew, though, that she wanted and needed more. Not because she felt incomplete, but because she longed to share herself, to love and be loved for herself. She'd never pretended not to want a man in her life, but she wasn't willing to settle for the wrong man. Not now. And not in the future.

When Patrick slipped his arm around her and drew her against his strong body, Bailey admitted another truth. She wanted to feel for that right man what she'd begun to feel for Patrick Sutton.

Looking up at him, she met his gaze. Her breath stopped for a long moment. The heat and desire in his eyes reflected the heated desire that flowed through her veins. Bailey trembled.

Patrick frowned. "Are you still afraid of me?"

Unable to summon a single word of denial, she shook her head. Didn't he realize the extent of his impact on her? she wondered as she stared up at him.

"What's wrong, then?" he asked.

I'm afraid of what I feel, she almost said. "Nothing's wrong."

"Bridges and islands time?"

She bit her lip in order not to laugh. She also

relaxed, which surprised her given the turmoil in her heart and body.

He turned her so that they were face-to-face. "You mystify me at times, Bailey Kincaid."

"That's not altogether bad, is it?"

"Makes for a lot of . . ." He paused, as if wrestling to find the right word.

"Confusion?" she supplied.

"Repressed desire," he said, correcting her even as he placed his hands on her waist and drew her nearer.

She stepped in to him, a shattered-sounding sigh slipping past her lips as her senses registered the feel of his powerful body. It was all she could do to think clearly.

He brought his arms around her, but he said nothing.

She felt the up-and-down sliding motion of his hands as he caressed her back from shoulders to hips. The silk of her dress proved to be a nonexistent barrier to the warmth of his hands. She edged a bit closer, unable and unwilling to resist the heat emanating from him or the sensuality of his touch.

"I had no idea that you were attracted to me," she said softly.

"You weren't supposed to know. I had, and still have, far too much respect for you to treat you like a potential conquest."

"Oh," she whispered.

With their bodies so closely aligned and her forehead resting against his chin, she fell prey to the sensations creating havoc inside her as she stood within the circle of his arms. She felt the flex and flow of his muscular body, felt as well the acceleration of his heartbeat the instant her breasts plumped against his hard chest. His sharply indrawn breath echoed in her ears. Seconds later arousal more acute than anything she'd ever felt before coalesced inside her and made her pulse leap into a gallop.

"I have to kiss you, Bailey," he confessed as he leaned down.

She lifted her face into view. Even as she searched his features for some hint of his emotions, she realized that she no longer cared about the world of illusion that he represented.

Neither did she care that they were standing in a public place. In truth, the world and all the people populating it seemed irrelevant. And, at that moment, Bailey cared even less about all the boundary lines she'd put in place against him.

What she cared about was the here and now, and the driving need storming inside her to know this man as intimately as possible. Despite all the valid reasons not to admit to herself that she was falling in love with him, she abandoned the pretense of indifference and stopped denying what she needed as his lips settled over hers. She would deal with the consequences of her surrender, she rationalized, only when she had to.

Angling her head and parting her lips, she welcomed him with the curious sense that she was somehow fulfilling her own destiny. The flavor of him was everything she'd imagined in those quiet moments just before dawn when she'd tantalized herself with speculations of his skill as a lover. In essence, Patrick Sutton was a fantasy come to life, the fantasy nursed by the romantic nature nearly destroyed by her divorce.

As he tenderly explored her lips she moaned low in her throat and twined her arms around his neck. She pressed against him, welcoming the muscular power of his body against her own smaller frame and the very telling evidence that he desired her just as much as she desired him.

He scavenged her senses and laid claim to her soul with his searching kiss. He gripped her waist with his hands, his fingers nearly spanning the narrow expanse as he brought her flush against his swollen loins. Whatever control he'd ever possessed disappeared like a puff of smoke as Bailey eagerly answered his passion with darting stabs of her tongue into the heat of his mouth.

He couldn't believe her responsiveness, but he was well beyond questioning it. He needed her too much, wanted her with a longing that had accumulated over several years. Stunning bursts of pleasure detonated within his body. A wave of almost reckless desire swept over and through his senses.

Patrick wanted to absorb her into his body and lodge her permanently in his soul. The primal urge to stake a claim on her nearly sent his desire skyrocketing out of control. It was all he could do not to shout to the world that this woman was finally his and she always would be.

He refused to consider the possibility that he might fail in his bid to capture her heart. He wouldn't tolerate failure where she was concerned, although he realized that he had a battle ahead of him. The past still cast a shadow across their future.

He needed to be patient, needed to help her work her way beyond her fear, but patience seemed a fragile thing as she shuddered in his arms and tangled her tongue with his. He tasted her sweet heat with shocked wonder, one of his fantasies about her becoming reality. She moved against him ever so subtly and oh so sensually, tantalizing him to imagine their bodies naked and joined in the ultimate passion.

The paging device he wore suddenly vibrated. Startled, Patrick gripped Bailey even tighter and damned every electronic invention ever manufactured. He ignored it until it vibrated a second time and Bailey went rigid in his arms.

He reluctantly released her lips, but he didn't reach for the pager. He held her shaking body, heard the uneven cadence of her respiration and his own. They both needed time to reclaim themselves, time to master the shattering desire that made them tremble and cling to each other.

He muttered a curse when the device vibrated yet again, then reached for it. With one arm still around Bailey, he glanced at the pager and saw that there was no message.

"Is it yours or mine?" she asked breathlessly, her head resting against his shoulder.

"It must be yours." Patrick knew he sounded as ragged around the edges as he felt.

Bailey slid her hand between their bodies, the knuckles of her fingers brushing across the washboard flatness of his abdomen. He sucked in a harsh breath, then slowly let it out, struggling to tamp down the arousal that had hardened his entire body.

"Sorry," she whispered.

"No problem."

Easing free of her, he watched Bailey fumble with the pager clipped to the belt of her silk dress. Her hands shook. As the small device began to slip from her fingers, he caught it and handed it to her.

"Thank you," she said, meeting his gaze. "I'm a little . . ." She cleared her throat. "Well, you know."

"I know. I am too." Patrick gently cupped her cheek, the heat from her skin penetrating his palm. "And you're welcome." He smiled, despite the urge he felt to grimace over his physical discomfort. "You're very beautiful."

She shook her head in a self-mocking way that he found endearing.

"What I am is disheveled. I also ache all over."

He grinned. "You're not alone."

Her gaze dipped brazenly, and she returned his grin. "Trust me, I'd already figured that out for myself."

Patrick fought the impulse to toss both of their pagers into the Pacific. He wanted her, wanted to make love to her until they were both too sated to move. And then he wanted to do it again, over and over, because he doubted that he would ever get enough of her.

Bailey released a sigh, squared her shoulders, and made her way to a spot beneath one of the light fixtures on the pier. She pressed a button on her pager. Patrick joined her, slipping his arm around her but not invading her privacy as she read the digital message.

He heard the words as she repeated them a moment later, but they didn't register. His thoughts were on the woman standing beside him, on the feel of her lush body as he'd held her, the sweet taste of her, and the hunger she hadn't tried to conceal from him. Bailey read the message a second time. He realized then that she was also having trouble digesting their meaning.

"Fox Ridge job vandalized. Guard missing. Meet me. Jeff."

Her voice sounded so hollow that it could have been mechanically produced. Patrick felt gut-punched as her words sank into his brain. He watched the glow drain out of Bailey's face until she looked ashen. When she turned on her heel and walked away, he muttered the foulest word he knew and followed her.

FIVE

Patrick caught up with Bailey as she reached her Jeep in the parking lot. He clamped a hand on her shoulder to stop her, but she shrugged free of him, jerked open the driver's-side door, and tossed her purse inside the vehicle.

"Wait, dammit!" he shouted as she started to climb into the Jeep.

She swung around to face him, fury in her vivid blue eyes. "Do not give me orders."

"You're not behaving rationally, Bailey."

"I'll behave any blasted way I please, so quit yelling at me."

Patrick consciously lowered his voice. "You can't drive in this condition. So take a minute and settle down."

"I'm fine," she insisted.

"Yeah, you're fine. You're so fine, you're shaking." He reached out to place his hands atop her shoulders, but she deflected them.

"Don't touch me again. You forfeited that right the moment I realized you've lied to me."

Her sharp tone sent a shaft of despair straight through his heart. He lowered his hands, but he didn't move away from her, nor did he bother to deny her accusation. "Tell me what you intend to do."

"Why don't you tell me the truth instead?" she challenged.

"What truth?" he demanded.

"It's obvious that someone doesn't want you to build at Fox Ridge. I want to know why."

"Bailey, I . . ." He paused, aware that he owed her an explanation but worried about how she would take the news that someone might be stalking him.

"My instincts told me that you were holding back on me that first day, but I ignored them. I will never do that again. No more lies of omission, Patrick, and no more clever sidestepping. I know that's your specialty, but I will not have it. I want the truth and I want it now."

He exhaled heavily. *Where do I start?* he wondered as he studied her.

"Time's up, Mr. Sutton." She climbed into the Jeep and reached for her seat belt.

Patrick swiftly circled around the vehicle, threw open the passenger door, and settled himself in the seat next to Bailey as she jammed the key in the ignition.

She gripped the knob of the stick shift and jerked it into reverse, but she kept her foot on the brake pedal. "Get out, Patrick. Now."

"Not in this lifetime."

"Damn you!" she cursed, glaring at him.

His expression bleak, he nodded. "Sometimes I believe I am."

She stared at him for several moments. He saw the confusion on her face, and—before she blinked it away—the concern. He took the latter as a positive sign.

He remained silent, however, as Bailey backed out of her parking space and exited the parking facility. She barreled down the narrow two-lane portion of the pier that led to the gate, slowed for a speed bump, then pulled into the flow of street traffic.

Patrick glanced in the rearview mirror and spotted his limo gliding along behind them. He took small comfort in the diligence of his driver, who apparently had no intention of being too far from his employer.

As Bailey drove he watched her. She emanated outrage, and he didn't blame her. He'd prayed that there wouldn't be any further incidents at Fox Ridge, but his prayers had been ignored. Now he prayed that no one had been injured, or worse.

Bailey's tension was apparent to Patrick at every red light and road sign that forced her to stop, but in spite of her anger she efficiently navigated the streets of the beach community. Once they reached Montecito, a sleepy enclave of estates that housed the rich and famous, the road narrowed and steepened, and she concentrated on guiding the Jeep up into the hills toward Fox Ridge.

"Are you willing to listen to what I have to say?" he finally asked her.

"You have a captive audience for another ten minutes."

Although her response was terse, Patrick didn't fault her. How could he? he asked himself as he rubbed the back of his neck in frustration.

"About six months ago some very strange things started happening at the Sutton Group offices in Beverly Hills. Taken separately, they could be explained away as simple accidents."

"Taken together?" she prodded.

"Taken together, they weren't as easy to write off."

"What happened?"

He reluctantly supplied some of the specifics. "Fires in trash cans, a computer virus that almost wiped out the accounting system, missing files that could have compromised the safety and security of clients and their families. That sort of thing."

"Did you call the police?"

"Not at first," he answered. "I resisted the notion that the incidents were connected. I didn't want to overreact, but I didn't want my employees jeopardized either. Most everyone at the agency has been with me since the beginning. They're incredibly loyal. To make a long story short, I contacted a private security firm, hired one of their investigators, and gave him carte blanche. He did background checks on the office staff, as well as on the people we do business with in the industry. He found nothing out of the ordinary. To be on the safe side, though, I had Jeanne hire a new cleaning crew, and the security firm sent over guards that were on duty from dusk until dawn. Things settled down for a while."

"For how long?" Bailey asked.

"Until I was in London for the premiere of Colette Bellamy's last film."

"*Midnight Storm*?"

"Yes."

"I liked it," she admitted, her tone of voice more even.

"So did I." Relieved that she seemed calmer, Patrick continued, "While I was gone two cars were set afire in the underground parking garage. It was a small miracle that no one was injured and the fire didn't spread to the offices upstairs. I was shown photos by the arson investigators once I returned, and it was obvious that someone had raised the stakes. I hired around-the-clock security, installed a key-card entry system, and had the police increase patrols around the office building."

"It didn't end there, did it?"

"Unfortunately, no. It was the calm before the next storm. Whoever is responsible for all this started targeting some of my key people in their homes. If I ever get my hands on the son of a—"

"What happened, Patrick?" she asked, interrupting him.

"Jerry Lindstrom was mugged in his garage after getting home late from a meeting, and Miriam Struthers almost drowned in her swimming pool when someone held her underwater. Jerry was knocked unconscious and didn't see the guy who attacked him, and Miriam was too disoriented to identify her assailant. That's when I decided to effect some major changes, changes I'd been considering for a variety of reasons, although I hadn't planned on instituting them for another five years or so."

"The move to Santa Barbara?"

"Exactly. I purchased an office building in downtown Santa Barbara six weeks ago. I'm relocating everyone who's willing to join me up here. For all practical purposes, a lot of people think of this area as Hollywood North. The transition starts in two weeks. I'd always planned to build a home at Fox Ridge. Now I've had to speed up those plans. In the meantime I have private security people monitoring all of my employees."

Bailey pulled off the paved road and onto the rutted lane at the entrance to Patrick's exclusive acreage. But instead of proceeding to the building site, she stopped the Jeep and set the parking brake.

"What about your clients?" she asked, still gripping the steering wheel and staring out at the darkness.

"They're all fine so far, but I'm worried about them for obvious reasons."

"You should have told me all this last week, Patrick."

"The simple truth is that I didn't want to believe the person responsible had followed me up here."

"Who hates you so much?" she asked as she shifted in her seat and faced him.

Patrick met her gaze, surprised that she was willing to talk to him. She was right, of course. He should have told her the truth, and he felt like a fool for not having done that before.

"Who, Patrick?" she pressed.

"I wish to hell I knew, but I don't have a clue."

"I can't allow Pete and his helpers to get caught in the cross fire."

"I understand how you feel."

A police cruiser pulled up beside them. Bailey waved a hand in greeting at the officer, then put the Jeep back into gear. "Jeff's waiting for me."

Patrick nodded, lapsing into silence as Bailey followed the cruiser up the winding road that led to the building site. Another glance in the rearview mirror told him that his limo was still right behind them.

Bailey spotted Jeff as she pulled into the clearing, the expression on his face warning her that he was furious. She scanned the drilling site and the area around it, her own frustration spiking yet again.

Several police officers armed with flashlights were searching the area around the disabled drilling rig for evidence. An older man in a uniform Bailey didn't recognize limped into view with the aid of an officer. Pete Higgins jogged over to help.

As she and Patrick climbed out of the Jeep, an ambulance, lights flashing, burst into the clearing and screeched to a stop. The two attendants jumped out and made a beeline to the limping man. They assisted him to the emergency vehicle. Because of his attire, Bailey assumed that the limping man was the retired police officer Jeff had hired as a security guard for the Fox Ridge site.

"Bailey, I need to talk to you now," Jeff shouted.

She nodded in his direction, then glanced at Patrick. "Why don't you give me a minute?"

Patrick gave her a look she didn't understand before accompanying her across the clearing. She knew her brother well enough to realize that his temper was on the verge of exploding. She didn't doubt her ability to handle the fallout. Patrick was another matter. Although she knew he wouldn't tolerate Jeff going off like a proverbial rocket, she still wasn't in the mood to witness a shouting match between the two men.

"Thanks for the call, Jeff. What have you found so far?" she asked in a no-nonsense tone that she used to remind her brother that *she* ran Kincaid Drilling.

"Enough to convince me that you're in way over your head, baby sister."

"Thanks for the vote of confidence." Her tone was so dry, it sounded like rustling leaves.

"This isn't about confidence."

She nodded brusquely. "No, it isn't. It's about damaged drilling equipment and an act of vandalism. The rest we can discuss later."

"Incident number four, if memory serves." Jeff shoved his fingers through the trademark Kincaid white-gold hair that topped his head.

Acting Police Chief Jeff Kincaid then stabbed his sister's companion with a look that would have leveled the average man. Bailey smiled when Patrick simply peered back at him.

"Who's your friend?" Jeff demanded.

Looking undaunted, Patrick extended his hand as he stepped forward. "Patrick Sutton. I own the property. Thanks for responding so quickly."

After a moment's hesitation, Jeff accepted his extended hand. "Jeff Kincaid, Santa Barbara Police Department. We have a problem here, Mr. Sutton, one I believe you're quite familiar with, considering what's been happening on your turf in L.A."

"You're thorough," Patrick acknowledged.

"Always," Jeff responded. "But especially where my sister and our company are concerned."

"I understand. How's the security guard?"

"He was roughed up and then shoved over the

side of the clearing. Luckily, he landed on a ledge. He radioed for help, and we found him twenty minutes later."

Bailey turned and studied the scene by the ambulance. The guard was being helped into the vehicle. "What are his injuries?" she asked.

"Cuts, bruises, and a sprained ankle, from what we can tell. We'll know more after he's checked out at the emergency room."

"Thank God for small favors."

"What about the drilling rig?" Patrick asked.

"He, or they, didn't have time to do much damage."

"Any footprints?"

Jeff's gaze narrowed. "A few possibles."

"Make sure I get all the bills for the guard's medical care and any damage done to the equipment."

"That can be arranged," Jeff agreed.

Bailey's gaze traveled between the two men. While she was relieved that Jeff hadn't lost his famous temper, she was deeply concerned about Patrick. He hadn't used the word, but she felt certain that he was being stalked. The very thought that someone wanted to hurt him sent a chill through her, as did the realization that her employees remained in jeopardy if she didn't abandon the Fox Ridge job.

When he spoke, Patrick's tone was as somber as his facial expression. "I want the job closed down, effective immediately. I won't build a new life for myself at the expense of other people's lives."

"I don't think we have any other choice," Bailey agreed. "My people have to be protected, and you need to rethink your plans."

He nodded. "I'm at the Biltmore if anyone needs to talk to me. Thank you all for what you've tried to do." Turning away from them, he made his way to the limo parked at the edge of the clearing.

Bailey didn't take her eyes off of Patrick until he climbed into the vehicle. Shoulders sagging in defeat, she gratefully accepted the hug Pete Higgins gave her as he joined them.

"He's not a bad fellow," Pete observed.

"He seems all right," Jeff conceded.

"He's a good man," Bailey said, her voice firm as she watched the limo disappear from sight.

"Lousy luck on this one, young lady, but closing down's the safest thing to do. We'll get to it first thing tomorrow."

"Thanks, Pete." She met her brother's curious gaze. "I don't like being manipulated, especially by someone cowardly enough to play games with other people's lives."

Jeff frowned at her. "Sutton may be an okay guy, but I don't want you within a hundred miles of him. This isn't negotiable, little sister. Are we clear on that?"

Bailey stiffened. "Don't, Jeff. I'm not in the mood for misplaced protectiveness." She shifted her attention to Pete. "Let's meet at the shop in the morning. I'll bring Charlie Cannon up to speed on what's happened."

"Sounds good to me." Pete ambled back to the drilling rig.

Bailey faced Jeff once more. "Can you assign someone to patrol the job site until Pete and his helpers can get a truck up here tomorrow?"

"It's already done. In the meantime I've got an evidence technician headed this way. He ought to be here fairly soon."

"I'm tired, so I'm going home. Why don't we talk later?" Bailey didn't wait for an answer. She simply turned and headed in the direction of her Jeep, her thoughts shifting back to Patrick and the worry she felt over his safety.

"Bailey!"

She paused to glance over her shoulder at Jeff.

"Are you all right?" he asked as he strolled toward her.

She managed a smile, unaware that it looked more like a grimace. "Nothing's wrong with me that a good night's sleep won't cure."

"What's going on between you and Sutton?"

She almost laughed. Jeff the bloodhound was back. "He's a client."

He spoke quietly then. "He seems to be more than that, baby sister."

She squared her shoulders. "He's Jeremy's agent."

"What else is he?"

He's someone who makes me feel and want in ways I

never thought possible, she realized, not for the first time. Tears swelled in her eyes, but she blinked them away as she met her brother's probing gaze. "He's just a man, Jeff."

"Coffee on the patio at six?" he asked.

She didn't question her good fortune at the out he gave her, although she knew he'd pick up where he left off at the first opportunity. "You've got a date."

"Is that where you were tonight? On a date with Sutton?"

"Does it matter one way or another, Jeff?"

"You haven't dated anyone since your divorce."

"You're right, I haven't." Smiling sadly, she turned and walked to her Jeep.

Bailey took a steadying breath before starting the engine. She ached with regret and a deep yearning, but she knew better than to torture herself with thoughts of what might have been. As the Jeep bumped along the rutted road she felt angry and powerless. Anger turned to surprise seconds later, when she spotted Patrick's limo parked at the entrance to his property.

She braked the Jeep when the passenger door of the limo swung open and Patrick emerged. Pulling over, she turned off the engine and climbed out.

"Do you have a minute?" Patrick asked as he took her arm and guided her around an uneven patch of ground.

"Of course." Curious as to why he'd waited for

her, she studied his features once they paused at the edge of the driveway and faced each other.

"I didn't intend for our evening to end this way," he began. "And I owe you an apology."

"I think you've got things a little backward. I'm the one who lost my composure at the pier."

"I still shouldn't have shouted at you. I had no right to do that. Nor did I have the right to hold back on the truth."

Bailey smiled. "You've met my brother, so you've probably figured out that a little shouting isn't going to turn my world upside down. As for holding back on the truth, I'm still wrestling with your motives," she admitted.

"Then I do owe you an apology," he insisted.

She asked the one question that dominated her thoughts and compromised her emotional balance. "Were you trying to manipulate me when we were at the pier?"

"Do you really think I'd do that to you?"

"Not deliberately. Look, you've made my point for me, so forget the apologies, all right? You have a much bigger issue to deal with at the moment."

He shook his head, but a hint of laughter added luster to his dark eyes. "You always make your own rules, don't you?"

She shrugged. "When it's necessary."

"I suspect that's probably why we get along so well."

"Don't forget the chemistry," she said, her tone of voice tart.

Patrick stepped closer and placed his hands on her waist. Bailey's breath caught in her throat as she looked up at him.

"What are you thinking right now, Bailey Kincaid?"

His voice was so low that she almost didn't hear the words, but not so low that she wasn't instantly caught up in the memory of the sensual exchange they'd shared less than an hour earlier. Despite the temptation he posed to her senses and her heart, Bailey forced herself to answer his question. "What I'm thinking is that I'm worried about you."

"Is that all?"

She knew he was teasing, but she didn't feel at all lighthearted. "I know how painful it can be when you're placed in the position of watching your dreams fall apart, especially since I now believe that the Fox Ridge house was more than a safe harbor against a stalker. You obviously want a real home."

"Precisely, but as you said earlier, I need to rethink my plans." He drew her even closer, his desire evident in the possessiveness of his touch.

She went willingly. She still wanted him, wanted him so fiercely that little else mattered at that particular moment.

He gathered her against his body, his arms tightening around her, his heavy sigh like an echo of the relief flowing through her. She sagged against him, savoring the strength and heat of him, savoring as well the sense of completeness she found in his embrace.

Despite his delay in telling her the whole truth, she silently forgave him. She knew firsthand about giving yourself false hope and believing that bad situations could somehow fix themselves. She even understood how a person could pretend that evil and cruelty didn't exist at all. She'd done that to her own detriment in the past. Sadly, she now knew that the real world was filled with every manner of person imaginable—including stalkers.

She slid her arms around his neck and held on tightly, terrified for his safety and equally terrified that her brother had unknowingly uttered some very prophetic words. She *was* in way over her head. In more ways than one.

As she looked up at Patrick, she knew what she needed—knew what he needed, as well. Her eyes fell closed as his lips settled over hers. Relief flooded her senses.

She parted her lips even more, welcoming him without hesitation or her legendary caution. And as he dipped his tongue into her mouth, she tasted the depth of their mingling need, need that threatened to obliterate common sense and reduce the world to a wonderland of erotic sensations too compelling to resist.

She embraced his passion as he embraced her, surrendering her defenses and making a gift of her desire. A car horn suddenly blared, shattering the moment and jarring them both back to reality.

Bailey flinched. Patrick wrenched his mouth free, swiftly turning her so that her back was to the approaching vehicle. He kept her sheltered in his arms, as she struggled to even out her respiration. She felt the hard ridge of flesh that pressed against her lower abdomen, and a gust of air shuddered out of her. She wanted him so desperately.

Once the vehicle entered the property and moved past them on the rutted dirt road, Patrick eased his hold on her. "You okay?" he asked.

Bailey heard the strain in his voice. Still overwhelmed by the force of their desire for each other, she simply nodded.

"You need to get yourself home," Patrick said.

She nodded a second time. He slipped his arm around her shoulders and walked her back to her Jeep. Pulling open the door without releasing her, he smiled down at her, but it was a strained smile at best. "Hell of an evening," he muttered.

She smiled weakly. "You could say that."

He gave her a wry look, then dropped a kiss on her forehead. "I just did."

"Adding humorist to your résumé?" She got into the Jeep as she asked the question, smoothing her shaking hands around the circumference of the steering wheel to steady them.

She glanced up at him, longing welling up inside of her as she scanned his hard-featured face and imagined what it might be like to have his lips and hands skimming over her naked body. Heaven, she concluded. Pure heaven. *God, help me*, she thought. *I don't care about the cost, I want him*.

Patrick leaned down and branded her lips with a hard little kiss that sent her senses spinning into space. When he finally drew back, she glimpsed his reluctance to let her go in the strained expression on his face. "There's nothing funny about the way I feel right now, but we need to get you home in one piece."

"Thank you, kind sir."

He smiled crookedly. "Drive carefully." He stepped back, waiting while she turned the key in the ignition. "Very carefully," he called out a second time as she eased out of her makeshift parking spot and onto the roadway.

Bailey glanced in her rearview mirror a moment later and saw him standing in the center of the road. She stuck her hand out the open window and waved before she rounded the curve.

As she drove Bailey reminded herself that no matter how much she wanted Patrick, he still remained a part of a world she loathed. How, she wondered, would she ever be able to reconcile his professional identity with the promises she'd made herself upon leaving Los Angeles? She couldn't, which left her with only one option. An affair.

But could she accept that kind of short-lived relationship when she wanted and needed more? Or was she kidding herself about her own tolerances?

Bailey slipped into bed nearly an hour later, all

the questions she'd asked herself during the drive home still winding through her head like endless miles of bad road. When she awakened just before dawn, she still hadn't found any answers. She wondered then if she ever would.

SIX

When Patrick arrived at her office the following evening at six, he found Bailey waiting for him on the patio. He didn't mince words. "I was surprised to get your message."

"I asked you here because there's someone I want you to meet."

He sighed in reluctance. A long day of meetings and no sleep the night before had taken a toll on him. "I don't think I'm really up for anything social right now."

"This is business, Patrick, and all you have to do is listen." She started to turn in the direction of her office on the opposite side of the patio.

He caught her by the hand and stopped her. "What's going on?"

"Trust me, all right?"

Although puzzled by her upbeat mood, he relented. "I do trust you, Bailey."

He really did, he realized, even though he felt
restless, on edge, and angry with the person intent
on turning his life and the lives of those people he
cared about into a living hell. He longed to forget
the entire situation, if only for a few hours. He
wanted to carry Bailey off to a quiet spot and sub-
merge himself in her passionate nature.

God, how he wanted and needed her, he
thought as he studied her upturned face. He realized that he still had to keep his feelings under
wraps, though. He had no other choice. She was
already skittish enough, and he worried over the
risks to her personally if the stalker suddenly got it
into his head to target her.

Bailey smiled at him. "You're sure you trust
me?"

Patrick frowned. "You know I do."

"Good. Then please come with me. You'll be
glad you did, I promise."

His gaze drifted over her, his response utterly
visceral as he took in the cropped tee and snug-
fitting jeans that covered her shapely body. He
couldn't help the hungry smile that briefly turned
up the edges of his mouth.

She lifted her free hand and stroked his cheek.
"You shouldn't look at me that way," she whispered.

He felt a slow burn taking place deep inside his
body at the gentleness of her touch. "You look
good enough to . . ." He paused, then exhaled un-

evenly as he tried to control his thoughts, not just his body's response to her.

She arched an elegant brow as she looked back at him. "You were saying?"

He couldn't make heads or tails out of her current mood, so he didn't bother to try. "Forget I said anything," he suggested, sounding as ragged as he felt.

"I have an interesting mental image, courtesy of what you didn't say."

He tugged her a step closer. The subtle scent of her perfume teased his senses. He kept his voice low enough not to be overheard by the person waiting for them inside. "Don't tempt me. I'm on a really short leash where you're concerned."

"Your restraint is duly noted and very much appreciated. Now, come on into my office," she encouraged. "Frannie's scheduled to deliver a speech at the university this evening, so she doesn't have much time for us."

"Frannie?"

"Francesca Reed. We've been friends since college."

"Francesca Reed of Reed International?" he questioned, familiar with her name and her work.

Bailey nodded. "That's Frannie."

As they entered Bailey's office a slender brunette got up from her chair and walked toward them. Patrick recognized her face, although he thought she was far more vibrant in person than in the photographs he'd seen of her that had graced the covers of various international periodicals during the previous ten years. The captions under the photos invariably read "beautiful and brilliant." Her beauty was obvious, but so was the intelligence in her assessing gaze when she removed her glasses and peered back at him.

Bailey made the introductions. "Patrick Sutton, I'd like you to meet Francesca Reed, my old college roommate."

Francesca Reed was a highly respected member of an exclusive international community of personal security specialists. Patrick realized, thanks to the reputation of her New York–based firm, that she served the security needs of several luminaries in the business, diplomatic, and film communities. At thirty-five, she was also an acknowledged authority on terrorism and had authored two books on the subject.

Patrick shook hands with her. "Your reputation precedes you, Ms. Reed."

She acknowledged his comment with shy smile. Patrick couldn't help wondering how many people underestimated her because of that smile.

"I know a little bit about the Sutton Group, thanks to some consulting work I did with the production company that handled the filming of *Midnight Storm*. Colette Bellamy speaks very highly of you," she said.

"Colette and her husband are good friends. I'm godfather to their twin boys."

Francesca nodded, then made her way across

the room to the conference table positioned in front of a set of closed French doors. "I understand from Bailey that you're being stalked, Patrick. Not an easy way to live, is it?"

"No, it is not," he conceded, his voice tightening with renewed tension. He joined the two women once they made themselves comfortable at the table.

"I've just received and have looked over copies of the police reports for the incidents that took place in Los Angeles, and I've spoken with the firm currently handling your security needs. After chatting with both Bailey and Jeff for a local update, I think I have a pretty clear picture of your situation."

Bailey chimed in when Frannie paused. "We went up to Fox Ridge this afternoon. Jeff met us there."

Patrick studied Bailey. "The job's been shut down, so there's no point in pursuing this. I don't want innocent people jeopardized for the sake of a house. In particular, I won't have you placed in danger by some crazy who's out to get me." His gaze shifted to Frannie. "We both know that there is no such thing as perfect security, especially if the stalker wants to strike again. My gut tells me he will, so we're at an impasse with this guy."

"Security is never foolproof, Mr. Sutton, but it can always be improved upon," Francesca said with the quiet confidence of someone who knew her business inside and out.

"I'd like to think you're right, but I still have serious reservations."

Frannie nodded. "I understand, of course, but I have some ideas. Would you be interested in hearing them?"

He glanced at Bailey, who smiled encouragingly at him. "Frannie understands dreams, Patrick. She understands them better than most people. Besides, I haven't had the equipment removed from Fox Ridge yet." Pausing for a moment, she straightened in her chair. "And I have no intention of being manipulated."

He didn't try to hide his surprise. Bailey had been absolutely adamant up to now about not placing her employees at risk. Why would she suddenly do an about-face? he wondered.

Unable to come up with an explanation for her altered attitude, he refocused his attention on Francesca Reed. "I'm always willing to listen, Ms. Reed."

"Then let's start with a possible profile of our stalker, which is based as much as possible on his actions to date," she said as she opened the leather portfolio on the conference table in front of her and removed a sheaf of handwritten papers.

Patrick settled back in his chair and listened with a more open mind than he'd have thought possible a short while earlier. Francesca Reed was nothing if not thorough, he quickly realized, and he understood why she was so highly regarded in her field. When she suggested that Tommy Dunlap's car accident needed to be investigated, Patrick's blood ran cold.

He no longer doubted the merit of reevaluating his perspective of the stalker and how to attempt to thwart him. He saw the risks, as well, but he felt assured that Francesca Reed and her staff were capable of dealing with them aggressively and efficiently.

At the end of their hastily arranged meeting, Patrick authorized Reed International to take over the task of safeguarding those people most jeopardized by the stalker's potentially life-threatening actions. He also made it clear that money was no object.

He knew he wouldn't stop worrying until the man was caught. He said a silent prayer that no one would be harmed in the interim.

As Francesca stood and reached for her purse she promised, "My people will be en route from New York within the next few hours. I have a reliable man in Los Angeles who'll take a hard look at Mr. Dunlap's vehicle, as well."

"I appreciate what you're doing." Patrick pushed up from his chair, extracted a business card from his wallet, and handed it to her. "Use my pager number when you call. You'll have direct access to me at all times."

"You'll hear from me in the morning. In the meantime please ask your driver to vary his routes until the driver I'm assigning to you arrives tomorrow morning, and say as little as possible to the people in your employ, even your executive assistant. I'll handle the explanations at your Beverly Hills office when I arrive there tomorrow. Simply ask Ms. Carson to call a meeting of the entire staff. Let her assume that you'll be present to orchestrate it."

"Agreed." He didn't doubt Jeanne's loyalty for a moment, but he was willing to play Francesca Reed's game her way.

Patrick saw relief in Bailey's remarkable blue eyes, but he thought he saw something more before she blinked it away. Although unsure of how to label her emotional state, he felt certain that she cared about his well-being. He smiled. "Thank you."

She inclined her head in that vaguely regal way of hers. "You're entirely welcome."

His attention lingering on Bailey, he realized that he no longer felt as frustrated or powerless as he had at the start of their meeting. He was a man accustomed to controlling his life and his world, so the events of the last six months had been a sobering experience.

As the two women crossed the room Patrick heard Bailey ask, "What about the situation with Jeff? Were you two able to clear the air?"

"Stop hoping for the impossible, Little Miss Fix-It. He's a stubborn man, and he's not about to change just because it would be the right thing to do."

"You're both stubborn, and you're both miserable."

"He knows my phone number in New York, so the ball, as they say, is in his court. Now, tell me where you found that sweater you were wearing this afternoon. I want you to get one just like it for me, but in garnet or jade," Francesca said as the wrought-iron gate clanged shut behind them and their voices grew muted.

Patrick remained in Bailey's office. *Little Miss Fix-It.* He smiled as helped himself to a snifter of cognac from a tray on an antique sideboard. He also poured one for Bailey, hoping that they could share a drink and some quiet time together after she finished walking her old friend out to the waiting cab.

He wandered around the spacious room, pausing every few feet to study the framed photographs on the walls, which chronicled the history of Kincaid Drilling.

As he walked he found himself questioning Bailey's willingness to set up the meeting with Francesca Reed. She'd gone above and beyond the call of duty. But then she always had, Patrick remembered. He'd sensed from their first encounter that when she cared, she fought for the person, especially if she perceived them to be the victim of an injustice. He'd learned that she fought with every tool at her disposal until the situation changed to her satisfaction. Patrick appreciated her sense of decency and fairness.

He realized that Bailey had taken up his cause, and the realization humbled and amazed him. It also gave him hope. Hope that she wouldn't rebuff the feelings he had for her once he revealed them. Hope that she'd eventually be willing to fight her own demons, if it meant that they could be together.

He didn't simply want her in his bed. He wanted much more from her. He was falling in love with her. Deeply. She possessed passion, integrity, and the strength of her own convictions, and he felt certain that she would be the perfect mate and ally as the future unfolded.

Patrick wondered if she would ever regard him in the same light. Would she believe his feelings for her? Would she be able to trust that they could share their lives?

He reminded himself once more not to press her too soon. She needed time and patience. And he needed her. He ached with the kind of need that told him that his heart had been on starvation rations for a very long time.

He turned at the sound of her footsteps, then watched her hesitate halfway across the room. Her wary demeanor prompted him to ask, "What's wrong?"

She shook her head, the gesture of denial sending a ripple through the white-gold hair cascading down her back. "Nothing's wrong, but there is something I want to tell you."

"I'm listening." He moved across the room, his

stride vaguely predatory, the desire he felt for her darkening his eyes.

Bailey shivered suddenly, then flashed a startled look at him. "Patrick."

He heard a note of warning in her voice. Pausing a few feet from her, he placed the brandy snifter on the coffee table beside him. He didn't take his eyes off of her. Not once. Not even to blink.

"Kincaid Drilling is staying on the job," she announced. "Frannie is sending two men who are qualified to work with Pete, in addition to the security personnel we'll need at Fox Ridge each night."

He nodded, his gaze fixed on the color steadily flooding her cheeks. "Are you feeling all right?" he asked.

She exhaled a gust of air and pressed her palms together in front of her. "Of course I'm all right." When he said nothing more, she asked, "Are you listening to me?"

Patrick smiled. "I'm listening. It occurs to me that I owe you more than a simple thank-you for everything you've done."

"You don't owe me anything." She started to walk to her desk.

Patrick caught her by the shoulder. "You amaze me."

"I thought I mystified you," she said, her words whispering over him like erotic sensations.

He smiled, the reason for her edginess suddenly dawning on him. Slowly and gently, he drew her forward into the heat and strength of his body. Desire flowed into his bloodstream like a molten river. "That too. Am I making you nervous?"

She planted both her hands against his chest to maintain the space that separated their bodies. "Don't be silly."

"I'm not letting go of you."

She went absolutely still in his arms. "You aren't behaving normally," she accused.

"Restraint probably isn't normal, now that you mention it," he mused thoughtfully.

She looked up at him. "Why are you restraining yourself?"

"You aren't ready."

"To make love?"

His eyes fell closed, and a ragged breath escaped him. Score one for Bailey, he thought, thrown off balance by her bottom-line question. "Exactly."

"Well, you're wrong."

Startled by her matter-of-fact tone, he peered down at her. "Say that again, please."

Bailey nodded. "Certainly. You're wrong."

He chuckled. "With a little less gusto, if you don't mind."

She reached up, slid her arms around his neck, and then brought his head down. With her lips only a few inches from his, she whispered, "You're wrong, Patrick Matthew Sutton. You couldn't be more wrong. I *am* ready."

"Thank you, God," he muttered before he hungrily claimed her lips and thrust his tongue into the sultry depths of her mouth.

She gasped, then moaned, the latter sound equal parts relief and surrender. He inhaled the seductive sound, basking in the sweet taste of her. She reminded him of a natural drug, and he couldn't imagine ever wanting to be cured of his addiction to her or the high she supplied.

As Bailey pressed against him he skimmed his hands up and down her back, then imprisoned her hips between his palms and let her feel the strength of his desire for her. He felt the answering tremor that moved through her, then the subtle uptilting of her pelvis. He shifted against her, his aroused body seeking that part of her designed to accommodate his throbbing flesh, despite the fact that they were both still clothed.

She tore her mouth free a few moments later. After a struggle to catch her breath, she managed two words. "Not . . . here."

Lifting her into his arms, Patrick cradled her against his chest. "Where?"

She looped her arms around his neck and rested her head against his shoulder. "My cottage."

He nodded and strode out of the office and across the patio. An open doorway and a muted light beyond beckoned. He followed the light and found her bedroom, not questioning the instincts that guided him because his entire being was centered on the woman in his arms.

Lowering her to stand in front of him, Patrick

met Bailey's gaze, once again marveling over the honesty of her desire for him.

As he started to unbutton his shirt she reached for the hem of her own, drew the garment from her body, and dropped it on the floor. Her bra, a delicate confection that revealed more than it covered, followed.

Unable to resist the temptation before him, Patrick paused after freeing his last shirt button. He reached out, cupping her high, full breasts in his hands, savoring the weight of them and the silken heat of her skin.

He heard Bailey suck in a sharp breath, and he felt her nipples tighten under his touch. Dropping to his knees in front of her, he fastened his lips to one taut knot of flesh and tugged at the other with his fingertips.

Bailey arched her back, then clutched at his broad shoulders. She whimpered faintly as he drew her nipple deep into his mouth and suckled it.

Pushing his shirt away from his shoulders with shaking hands, she kneaded the muscular expanse. She reminded him of a jungle feline, strong yet vulnerable, wholly desirable, but also capable of expressing her own desire.

As he sucked and nipped at her he realized that she tasted like wild honey. The flavor intoxicated his senses and seduced him even more.

Shifting his attention to her other breast, Patrick lavished it with the same loving attention. He feasted on her at length, drawing inarticulate murmurs and breathless little cries of surprise and pleasure from her. He loved every sound she made, and he absorbed the essence of each one for leisurely reflection later.

He enjoyed taking his time with her, indulging her, because he sensed from her almost shocked responses that no one had ever thought to put her first. He craved the distinction of being the one man capable of taking her to heights she'd never experienced before. He vowed to be that man, regardless of the cost of the control he now exerted over himself.

When she drove her fingers into his hair and tugged gently, he reluctantly withdrew his mouth from her breasts. He looked up at her, noticing that the illumination of the bedside lamp cast a glow across her golden skin. She was exquisite, so exquisite that she eclipsed all the women he'd ever met.

Despite the primitive possessiveness of the impulse, Patrick staked a mental claim on Bailey as they stared at each other in the semidarkness of her bedroom. And he silently promised himself that she would never need or want another man. Not ever.

"You're staring at me," she said as she swayed unsteadily.

He responded to the need within himself to caress her breasts, molding and shaping them with skillful hands. "You interrupted me. I hope you have a good reason," he said with mock solemnity.

Once he lowered his hands, she crossed her

arms over her breasts. Patrick's heart skipped a few beats at her shy yet innately erotic pose.

Bailey sighed. "As good as that felt, I can't stand up much longer."

Grinning, he pushed up to his full height, brushed her hands aside, and drew her into a loose embrace. She shivered repeatedly as he held her, but not because she was chilled, he realized. Every shiver was a statement of her arousal.

"Is that better?" he asked.

Laughing at his question, she lifted her arms to wrap them around his neck. He ground his teeth together as her hard nipples penetrated the mat of hair covering his chest. Like tiny daggers, they tantalized him and sent his senses into freefall. He groaned, the sound coming from deep within his soul.

"Problem?" she asked, twisting slowly from side to side in such a way that she caressed him with her entire body.

Setting her back a step, Patrick took a ragged breath, then shrugged out of his shirt before reaching for the fastening of her jeans. "A huge problem."

"Shame on you. You're bragging."

He said nothing, although he gave her a look guaranteed to scorch. He leaned over her to ease her jeans and panties free of her hips and down her thighs. She shifted her stance. The garments slid the rest of the way down her shapely legs. She stepped free of the puddled fabric and kicked it aside without breaking eye contact with him.

She observed him with corresponding intensity as he shed the rest of his clothing. "Oh, my," she whispered as he stood before her, one very naked, muscular male who took pride in maintaining a healthy body.

He felt the heat of her gaze as it roamed over him. He saw surprise and appreciation and a myriad of other emotions in her eyes. It was all he could do not to seize her and toss her onto the bed.

"You weren't bragging, were you?" She glanced up at him, so wide-eyed that he almost laughed for the joy he felt.

Smiling, he bit back a groan of pure physical anguish. His sex surged with response to her question, but he didn't say anything. He was too busy struggling for control. Patrick studied her, instead.

He'd imagined what she might look like, but he wasn't prepared for the voluptuousness of her hourglass-shaped figure. He took in the nothingness of her waist and the flaring width of her hips. Her stomach was flat and her legs possessed the exquisite symmetry and tone of an experienced runner's. He'd admired them before, and now, in his mind's eye, he imagined them wrapped around his hips.

He closed his eyes for a moment, waiting for the image to fade, waiting, as well, to be able to control the impulse that urged him to take her before he went up in flames.

He felt her touch as she cupped the side of his face with her hand. "I always talk too much when I'm nervous. I just don't want to disappoint you, Patrick."

Turning his head, he pressed a kiss into her palm before opening his eyes and looking down at her. "You couldn't disappoint me. Not ever. Despite your advanced years, you, Miss Bailey Kincaid, are the nearest thing to perfection I've ever seen." He fitted his hands around her waist and brought her hips flush against his swollen loins. He shuddered at the contact, and he fought yet again for the control he needed in order to go slowly with her.

Bailey's eyes fell closed. She rocked against the hard ridge of flesh trapped between their lower bodies while also slipping her arms around him and pressing a series of stinging little kisses across his neck. "I'm glad you approve."

As he leaned down to claim her mouth Patrick assured her, "I more than approve." *I love you*, he finished in the silence of his mind. *I love you more than life itself, and someday soon I'll tell you.*

"Me too."

He nipped at her lower lip. "And I don't intend to disappoint you. Not ever."

"Somehow," she whispered against his lips, "I think I've known that all along."

He led her to the bed, then lowered her onto it before dropping down to recline on his side next to her. Gazing down at her, he trailed his fingers up her thighs, around the nest of silk that shielded secrets, over her quivering belly, and across each of her breasts.

Sprawled on her back in one instant and then turning in to him a heartbeat later, she whispered, "I want you so much, Patrick."

He knew then that the teasing and the games were over. She didn't need them anymore. She needed him. Sensing that she also needed the freedom to make her own discoveries about him, he willingly let her set the pace.

Bailey fused her lips to his as she surged against him. Arms locked around her, he imprinted the lushness of her warm body onto his senses as he skimmed his fingertips over her silken skin from shoulders to hips.

Angling her head, she tangled her tongue with his, taunting and teasing until he thought he might go insane. Her hands moved over every part of him that she could reach, her touch provocative and curious at the same time. He gave Bailey the access she sought, enduring the scorching strokes of her fingertips as she traced white-hot streaks of sensation across his flesh. He, in turn, explored her like a mapmaker intent on charting terrain he had already claimed as his own for all eternity.

When she shifted her hand between their bodies and measured the length and thickness of his arousal with her fingers, he jerked under her touch, endured it for as long as he could, then wrenched free of her. He turned the tables on her in the next instant. Rolling her onto her back, he came down atop her and smoothed the tangled white-gold strands of hair from her face.

She looked up at him, confusion and desire clouding the blue of her large eyes. "Why did you stop me?"

"I need a minute," he said roughly. "So do you, for that matter."

"I need *you*," she insisted, "and I know you need me."

He wanted to be absolutely certain that she knew her own mind. This wasn't some sexual hit-and-run accident. He wanted it to be a beginning for them, not some interlude that could be discounted after the fact. And he didn't want her to regret what they were about to share, even if it meant denying himself and giving her more time.

"What is it, Patrick?" She framed his face with her hands, her confusion evident.

"Are you absolutely sure that this is what you want?" he asked.

Bailey smiled, but tears flooded her eyes.

Alarmed, he gathered her close and held her. "Talk to me, love. Tell me what you're thinking."

She pressed a kiss to his neck, then hugged him. "I couldn't be more sure of anything, so please don't worry that I'll regret this, because I won't."

He eased her back down so that he could see her face. As he looked at her he saw the certainty in her gaze. He also saw a wealth of emotion, emotion that he allowed himself to think might be love, or, at the very least, some form of it. "I believe you."

"You should," she told him.

"Once won't be enough," he warned, although he didn't take the cautionary statement any further.

She gave him a watery grin, the irreverent side of her nature making an appearance. "I certainly hope not."

Patrick rolled onto his back seconds later. He took Bailey along for the ride, and she wound up sprawled across his chest. He slowly brought her up the length of his hair-roughened body, his gaze on her expressive features the entire time.

He knew by the look on her face that she realized his intent. He interpreted her smile as assent. Once she was kneeling astride his shoulders, he drew her into the heat of his mouth by guiding her hips with gentle hands. He felt the trembling of her entire body, and he knew then that she welcomed what they were about to share.

He gave to her then, his mouth settling over her, his tongue stroking the already moist cleft of her body as she gripped the headboard of the bed. She gasped with shock, but she didn't pull away.

If anything, she sank against him in invitation as a shaken exhalation spilled past her lips. He explored her delicate flesh, painting the swollen folds with his desire and love for her. He sensitized her with every lingering stroke of his tongue. Savoring the taste of her, he sipped at the very essence of her femininity until she shook with near violence. He branded her even as he consumed her, an almost relentless edge to his quest to devastate her senses.

Her responsiveness as she trembled and quaked and cried out his name became his reward, but he didn't stop there. He drove her closer and closer to climax in the minutes that followed, then pushed her beyond the brink when he tucked two fingers into the searingly hot channel of her sex.

Bailey groaned her pleasure. A delicate network of interior muscles quivered around his fingers as she came apart. She gasped for breath in the aftermath of what turned into a sustained release. The tension that had seized and held her body in thrall eased ever so slowly.

Patrick aided her as she regained her sense of the here and now, his mouth still on her, but only to soothe. When he realized that she was on the verge of collapsing, he drew her down the length of his still-aroused body and gathered her into his arms.

He embraced her, his hands moving in a circular motion up and down her back as she rested her head against his chest. Although his own body demanded release, he made himself wait.

Bailey stirred a short while later. Lifting her head, she peered at Patrick. "You're sneaky."

He laughed at her accusation. "And you taste like wild honey."

Her mouth formed an O of surprise. Hands flattened against his upper chest, she pushed herself up so that she was seated astride his hips. Patrick caught her and held her still when she started to shift backward.

"It's my turn," she finally said, pushing his hands away.

He watched as she positioned herself so that she could kneel on the bed at a point level with his hips. Unable to resist, he reached out and trailed his fingertips over her pebble-hard nipples.

She shivered as she looked at him. Then she smiled.

It was the kind of siren's smile that promised retribution of the most sensual kind. "Something tells me I'm in big trouble."

She glanced at the part of his body that was closest to her, and then asked much too innocently, "Why would you think that?"

SEVEN

Bailey's appreciative gaze traveled the length of Patrick's leanly muscled body. Her hands followed her visual survey, and she felt the musculature of his body flex and flow beneath her fingertips as she slowly stroked him. Like a sightless woman intent on learning everything about her lover's body, she closed her eyes and committed him to memory through her sense of touch.

She caressed him over and over again, fascinated by both the sculpted contours of his anatomy and his response to her. When she finished, she knew every bit of him, from the curving shape of his calf muscles to the washboard flatness of his abdomen to the moon-shaped scar on his left shoulder.

Patrick gripped the sheet beneath him with both hands as she explored and caressed him. A fine sheen of sweat coated his warm skin. When Bailey combed her slender fingers through the coarse nest of hair that surrounded his maleness, he hissed a low curse, but the word sounded more erotic than offensive as it escaped him.

She paused and glanced up at him. "You sound as though I'm torturing you, Patrick."

"Aren't you?" he rasped.

"Never," she whispered as she clasped him between her palms and leaned forward. She exhaled, her breath washing across him.

He shuddered. "You're sure about that?"

"Well, maybe just a little," she admitted, her conscience getting the best of her. She wanted to devastate him as thoroughly as he'd devastated her a short while ago.

As she took him into her mouth she heard him draw in a harsh-sounding breath, then another one soon after. She immediately registered the pulse raging wildly beneath the smooth surface of his skin as she circled the head of his engorged flesh with her tongue.

Motivated by a desire to do nothing more than give him pleasure, she stopped worrying about her limited experience and allowed herself to be guided by her instincts. She also felt freer to reveal her deeply sensual nature than she had in years as she made love to Patrick.

She tantalized and she taunted, offering to him the same generous gift he'd given to her. She took her time. She explored. She experimented. And she discovered, through even the most subtle of his reactions, that she pleased and periodically shocked him.

Along the way Bailey expressed the depth of her love for Patrick without saying a single word. She wondered, but only briefly, if he realized the extent of her feelings for him. A part of her longed to tell him, but another part, the part that housed her anxiety that the past might somehow repeat itself, knew it was better that he didn't have a clue about the complexity of her emotions for him. She had yet to come to terms with them.

Banishing her troubling thoughts, she deliberately surrendered to the sensuality of their lovemaking. She just as deliberately put aside every other concern. She was tired of the past, and she didn't want to dwell on a future over which she knew she had little control.

She focused on the here and the now. That's all that counted, she told herself as she labored lovingly to force Patrick beyond the boundary of his self-control.

She knew she'd succeeded when a fierce-sounding groan tore free of him soon after. With no warning whatsoever, Patrick pushed up from the bed, caught her under the arms, and tumbled her onto her back. "You're killing me," he said, moving over her and settling his hips between her parted thighs.

Seizing her wrists, he dragged them above her head, shackled them together under the pressure of one hand, and used the other to brace his upper body weight so that he wouldn't crush her. He leaned down and drew the tip of one breast into his mouth.

Bailey felt the sensation caused by his marauding tongue and lips arrow directly to the core of her body. She arched her back and shifted her hips, instinctively seeking completion. Every cell in her body sang out its need for Patrick.

He shifted his attention to her other breast, alternately teething and sucking at the nipple until she felt like screaming her pleasure. When he freed her hands, she clutched at his shoulders.

"I want you inside me," Bailey pleaded. She felt his sex surge against the entrance to her body in response to her bold statement.

"Now, love?" he asked as he released the taut bud and raised his head to look at her.

"Now," she whispered.

He nodded, his dark eyes riveted on her as he penetrated her in one smooth motion. He didn't pause until he filled her completely. He held perfectly still in the moments that followed, allowing her to accustom herself to his size.

She exhaled shakily, her body quaking with pleasure. Streamers of sizzling sensation unfurled within her. "Yes. Oh, yes," she moaned.

He withdrew partway, then drove into her, over and over again until she was breathless. She met each of his powerful thrusts with an answering twist of her hips. And as she writhed and trembled beneath him her inner body tugged demandingly at his flesh.

Claiming her mouth and plunging his tongue into it, Patrick inhaled the frantic sounds she uttered as they made their journey together. She gripped his hips as he surged into her, her nails scoring his skin but not in a hurtful way.

An odd kind of tension began to tighten deep inside her body. It escalated until she felt like an overwound timepiece. She thrust upward, seeking, searching for, and welcoming the impaling force of Patrick's maleness as he repeatedly speared into her. His tongue stabbed into her mouth, duplicating the motion of his lower body.

Her release happened with a suddenness that knocked her off balance. It hurtled her into a glittering orbit of sensations that severed her hold on reality. She cried out, stunned by the extent of the climax that rolled over her like a fireball.

Clinging to Patrick, her body shook beneath his until she flirted with a loss of consciousness. He followed her just seconds later, his loins hammering against hers until he stiffened suddenly.

She felt his essence jet hotly into the depths of her still-trembling body as his orgasm claimed him. She held him, savoring the intimacy they shared.

Had anyone ever told her that she was destined to fall in love with Patrick Sutton, she would have laughed disdainfully and dismissed the notion as ludicrous. But she *had* fallen in love with him. Deeply. Desperately. He was everything she wanted in a man, but he represented much of what she feared, as well.

She sighed unevenly, the melancholy feeling in her heart blending with the lingering aftershocks that still moved through her body. Tears stung her eyes, but she quickly blinked them back. Patrick didn't need to know how conflicted she felt, and she certainly didn't want to admit the truth aloud.

He roused himself a few minutes later. As he drew her against his chest and rolled them onto their sides, he managed to say, "I've waited so long for you, Bailey Kincaid."

She burrowed against him, suddenly needing his strength to counter the anxiety she felt, if only until the dawn arrived. This was their time, she decided. Once again, she refused to allow anything else—especially the reality of their respective lives—to intrude on them, but she knew that she couldn't hold all of her worries at bay forever.

With their bodies still joined and their limbs tangled, they both drifted off. Fatigue gave way to renewed desire several times that night.

Bailey denied neither herself nor Patrick any sensual indulgences as she succumbed, heart and soul, to her hunger for him. They teased each other endlessly. They delighted and surprised each other, making love until they could barely move. Bailey knew in her heart that they shared a night of sensuality and eroticism that few people ever experienced.

Shortly before dawn, Patrick and Bailey forced

themselves from her bed. Both had busy days ahead. Bailey made a pot of coffee while Patrick showered. They shared a mug of the steaming brew as she bathed and he shaved. Even the naturalness with which they navigated the small bathroom together stopped surprising her after a few minutes. It seemed a natural extension of their night of intimacy.

Once he'd dressed and she pulled on her robe, they made their way to the front door of the cottage as the morning sun appeared high in the sky. Patrick dropped a hard and very possessive kiss on her lips before stepping outside. "I'll call you later today."

"I might be difficult to reach," she cautioned "I'll be on the run for most of the day."

He smiled like a rake, the fact that he was undaunted by any challenge evident in the expression on his hard-featured face. "I don't plan to misplace you now that I've found you again."

Her answering smile slipped little as she stood in the open doorway and watched him cross the patio. She lingered there even after he disappeared from sight, reflecting on the sensual nature of the man who owned her heart.

As she listened to the limo door slam shut and the sound of the engine turning over, she suddenly remembered the stalker and the potential jeopardy to Patrick's life. Even though Frannie's people were now protecting him, she whispered, "Please

God, take care of him," before returning to her bedroom to dress for work.

Patrick's remark that he'd waited a very long time for her flashed through her mind a short while later. The thought was displaced as she mentally went through the list of drilling sites that needed her attention.

As it turned out, Bailey missed Patrick's phone call at lunchtime. She learned that he called her two subsequent times—between meetings, according to her secretary—but her cellular phone was on the fritz and he was unable to get through to her. She considered the faulty cell phone a mixed blessing.

Although she never really knew what triggered it, Bailey started to question her own common sense by the middle of the afternoon. Was she crazy? Had she totally lost her wits? What did she think she would accomplish by becoming emotionally entangled in a relationship with Patrick Sutton? Nothing but heartache, she reluctantly concluded.

Self-doubt about her ability to completely trust any man plagued her, as well. Serious self-doubt. The kind of doubt that made mincemeat out of her confidence in her own judgment. Even though she told herself to quit being such a pessimist, she knew it would take a huge leap of faith on her part to place her happiness in the hands of another person. She honestly didn't know if she possessed the strength or courage to do it.

Bailey realized that she had some serious questions to ask herself, despite how much her time with Patrick the night before meant to her. She knew herself too well. An affair would leave her feeling self-destructive and in a lot of emotional pain.

Even though she felt like a coward, she turned off the ringer on her telephone and let the answering machine take Patrick's repeated calls. She reached the real bottom-line question that she needed to ask herself late that night, having avoided every attempt Patrick made to reach her by phone.

Was she willing to settle for an affair with Patrick, since nothing else seemed feasible?

Bailey knew she had to answer that question before she saw him again. Only then would she know for sure if she could move forward in their relationship. A relationship without a future.

She successfully dodged his calls for the next two days, but she knew she was living on borrowed time. A confrontation was inevitable, and in the end, it was Patrick who forced the issue when he showed up at her office.

Alone in the large room she was in the process of inspecting time cards before she sent them to the accountant. She froze when she heard Patrick's sensual voice.

"How about a late dinner?"

She looked up from the time cards. Clad in a

designer suit, he looked too desirable for words. He also looked worn-out and angry. She knew he had every right to be.

She felt her heart skitter to a stop, then resume beating at a high rate of speed. Her fingers itched with the need to touch him, so she closed them into fists and kept her expression neutral. "I'm not finished with work, so I'll have to pass."

He tugged loose the knot in his tie, unbuttoned the top two buttons of his shirt, and massaged the back of his neck. "I can have something delivered, if you'd prefer."

"No need," she said, trying to sound casual. "Since it's so late, maybe you should order room service at your hotel."

"I'll wait until you're ready to take a break."

The implacable expression on his face and his curt tone of voice assured her that he would wait her out until hell turned into a glacier, if that's what it took. Bailey saw no point in delaying the inevitable. "I can finish these later. Would you like a drink?"

He shook his head. "No, thanks. I noticed a Chinese restaurant on lower State Street the other day. Is it any good?"

"Yes," she answered. "But I'm not very hungry."

His gaze traveled over her. "You don't look as though you've been eating regularly."

She hadn't been. "I haven't had a lot of spare time the last few days."

He scanned her features. "Your nights haven't

been much better, have they? You don't look as if you've gotten much sleep."

She shrugged, but the tension already mounting inside of her escalated. "I can always catch up later. I've been awfully—"

"Busy," he finished for her, the word sounding like a curse as he said it. "Trust me, I know."

"Patrick, this really isn't a good time."

"Will there ever be one? Or are you going to avoid me until I give up on you and fade into the proverbial sunset?"

Bailey paled. She gripped the stack of time cards on her desk and told herself to stay in her chair, despite the urge she felt to jump up and flee.

"You cannot spend your future living in fear of your own emotions, Bailey. That kind of behavior destroys a person's spirit." He jerked his tie free of his shirt collar, wadded it into a ball, and shoved it into a pocket.

"Don't lecture me. You have no right."

"I have every right," he insisted, his temper flaring. "The night we spent together gave me a lengthy list of rights where you're concerned."

The time cards she held fluttered out of her fingers. Her innate honesty forced her to admit, "I'm still afraid, Patrick."

"Of me?" he asked quietly.

She slowly pushed herself to her feet. Her chin came up a few inches. "Of what I feel when we're together."

"So you're going to let your fear paralyze you?"

"I'm trying to figure out what to do."

"About us?"

She nodded.

"Then talk to me," Patrick urged.

"I'd rather work this through on my own."

"This is day four of your new recluse mode. How are you doing with your one-woman campaign to rationalize me right out of your life?"

His sarcasm hurt. "That's not what I'm doing," she protested.

"Isn't it?"

"Of course not."

"Then talk to me," he repeated.

"What's the point?"

"I'm half of the equation," he reminded her. "Don't I have a say in what happens between us and to us?"

"This isn't just about us. We're part of a larger picture," she said.

"What happens if I give it all up? What if I sell the Sutton Group agency to the highest bidder and take up bird-watching as a hobby for the rest of my life? Will that make you feel less threatened?"

"You can't do that!" she exclaimed, horrified at the thought that he'd even consider such a move.

"It would make you feel safe," he reminded her. "Since that's what you seem to need, why shouldn't I do it?"

She hated how insecure his solution made her sound, even if it was the truth. "It wouldn't be fair. You'd wind up hating me."

"I'll never hate you, Bailey, but neither will I abandon my professional relationships or commitments, any more than I'd expect you to do that for me. It's not reasonable or rational."

She pressed her fingertips to her temples. "I know all that."

"What about a compromise?" As he spoke he shrugged free of his suit jacket, draped it over the back of a nearby chair, and rolled up his shirtsleeves. He looked like what he was—a power broker settling in for a long session at the boardroom table.

She studied him with a wary expression. "Negotiation, you mean."

He laughed, but it wasn't a happy sound. "It's my specialty, and it's not a dirty word in most circles. But first, why don't you tell me your terms?"

Terms? "I just need some time, Patrick."

"Damn it to hell, Bailey, that's the last thing you need." He circled around her desk.

She put out her hands to deflect his advance. "Don't, please."

He ignored her plea and her attempt to stop him. Brushing aside her hands, he seized her by the shoulders and studied her.

Trembling beneath his touch because her senses remembered what it felt like to have his hands on her naked body, she noticed the blending of regret and frustration in his dark eyes as she looked up at him. "This isn't smart."

"You want an affair, don't you?" he broke in

before she could say anything else. "Something short, sweet, and very hot. The kind of no-emotions-involved, no-strings-attached liaison that consenting adults have when they're too busy or too disinterested in creating something solid and lasting with another person."

Her jaw dropped. She stared at him.

"I'm not a fool, Bailey, and you're so transparent some of the time that I feel like I'm looking through glass."

"Is an affair what *you* want?" she whispered.

His fingers tightened on her shoulders. "What do you think?" he demanded.

"I don't know what to think any longer," she confessed, not fighting him as he drew her against him and put his arms around her. "What's worse is that I'm afraid that I'll always feel the need to hold back a part of myself in any relationship in order not to be hurt."

"That's no way to live, Bailey."

"I know," she whispered, "but I don't know how to stop the feeling."

"Then let me help you get past it."

She shook her head. "You can't do that for me, Patrick, and you know it as well as I do."

As she gripped his waist she imagined her life without him. She saw a gaping hole and emptiness. She heard his ragged exhalation, and she knew she'd hurt him with her cowardice.

They stood that way for several silent minutes, together in one sense, but separate in another. Bailey felt overwhelmed by the emotions playing havoc with her heart. She wondered what Patrick was feeling, aside from his obvious frustration with her.

He released her unexpectedly, stepping back a pace so that they were face-to-face again. "You want me. I can feel it every time I get near you. It's also in your eyes when you look at me, and it emanates from your body like the heat from a lighted torch."

"Of course I want you," Bailey cried, exasperated because she felt almost crazed from desire for this man. "Wanting you is what's making this situation so complicated. Wanting you is making it impossible for me to think clearly, which is what I need to do."

Shaking his head, Patrick pivoted, crossed the room, and grabbed his suit jacket on his way to the French doors that opened out onto the patio.

Shocked and unable to keep silent, she asked, "Where are you going?"

He slowly turned around to look at her. "As much as I want you, I can't change who I am or what I do for a living. I also can't make a gift of the confidence you seem to lack. If I'm around you much longer, then I run the risk of taking advantage of you, and I don't want to do that. Believe it or not, I care very deeply about you, but I don't suppose that matters, since you haven't bothered to express an ounce of curiosity about my feelings for you."

He was right, she realized, slightly stunned by his last remark. But in her own defense, she didn't read minds. How in the world was she supposed to know how he felt? she wondered frantically. She still wasn't even sure what he wanted from her.

"Say something, Bailey, or I'm leaving here before I do something I may live to regret."

"Like what?" she demanded, feeling reckless.

"Like hauling you into your bedroom and making love to you until you come to your senses."

She recovered quickly from her shock. "Do it then! Take advantage of me!" she suddenly burst out, her self-control gone.

"Say that again," he ordered, his disbelief apparent.

"You heard me," she shot back. Her heart raced so fast, she felt faint. "If you do, then just maybe I'll be able to get you out of my system once and for all." *Liar!* her conscience shrieked. *What a liar! You'll never forget him. Not ever.*

Patrick smiled then. He just stood there and smiled at her.

Unnerved and uneasy, she realized that she'd just crossed some invisible boundary line with Patrick. She knew, as well, that she'd probably sounded like a borderline hysteric as she'd shouted at him to take advantage of her.

She met his gaze. Panic threatened even as she wondered what he was thinking. A second later she decided she was better off not knowing.

Casting aside everything but her desire for him,

she held her breath and waited to see what he would do. She waited all of ten seconds.

Patrick moved toward her like a predator accustomed to mastering every creature in the jungle. Bailey suddenly felt like his prey. Willing prey, she admitted to her conscience. Oh, so willing.

He reached for her, swept her off her feet, and brought her up to cradle her against his chest. Twining her arms around his neck, she stopped thinking after that. Although she silently vowed that when she was able, she would be supremely rational and resolve even the most unresolvable of her problems.

"I need you now, Bailey," he said as he lowered her to stand in front of him beside her bed and framed her face between his palms. "I need you every bit as much as you need me."

With his words echoing in her head, her hands shook as she hurriedly disrobed. Patrick shed his clothing just as swiftly, then tumbled her onto the bed. His mouth found hers an instant later, and she moaned both her relief and her hunger for him.

She lost all sense of time and place as he pitched her directly into an inferno of sensations too diverse to name. She met his passion with her own incendiary need, her mouth avid under his, her hands traveling over him as she refamiliarized herself with the glorious feel of his muscular body.

His arousal was immediate, his hunger for her evident in every erotic caress to her body. He touched her like a man denied tactile freedom for centuries, and he drank from her lips like a man who'd been abandoned in the desert.

Bailey basked in the aggressiveness of his passion. She responded in kind, too intent on expressing her love for him to employ any restraint. When Patrick traveled the length of her body, using his lips and tongue and teeth to stake his claim on her, she writhed helplessly on the bed.

He was so relentlessly thorough in his devotion to her pleasure that when she climaxed the first time, she wept as her body convulsed. She became the instrument through which he expressed his passion. He held her close each time he pushed her into the glittering abyss, his tenderness nearly her undoing.

Once she regained her strength, she set about offering the same heart-stopping sensory delights. She surprised him. She intrigued him as no other woman ever had. And she repeatedly tested his self-control, all the while totally dedicated to his pleasure.

He stopped her when she'd pushed him to the edge more times than either one of them could count, but instead of ceasing her erotic torment, Bailey shifted atop his body.

She mounted him, her hips poised just above his loins, her waist-length hair cascading past her shoulders and over her upper torso like a cape of white-gold threads. She looked wild and untamed.

He covered her breasts with his hands. She arched her back, loving the way he caressed her.

She heightened his arousal with the sensuous dance that followed, and his maleness grew slick with the heated dew of her body. She lured him and threatened his control, sliding against him again and again until he seized her hips and stopped her.

"More torture?" he demanded through gritted teeth.

Bailey smiled then. It was the slow, scintillating smile of a siren, and Patrick knew he'd remember it for the rest of his life. She sank onto him without warning, impaling herself with his hardness. He sucked in a harsh breath. She groaned, and the delicate muscles that surrounded his sex quivered wildly.

He fought for control in the moments that followed, his hands still bracketing her waist. He didn't try to stop her when she began to rock against him, though. He shuddered as she drew him in and out of her inner body with the subtle shifting and tilting of her hips and pelvis.

They shared the ultimate erotic mating dance as their bodies blended, the only sound in the room the gasping breaths they took.

When Bailey bent forward at the waist and clutched at his shoulders, Patrick wrapped his arms around her and captured her lips with his own. Submerging himself in the erotic fire of their mutual quest for fulfillment, he relinquished the last vestiges of his control. His heartbeat deafened him. Heat scorched his bloodstream. And the sense that he'd finally found an emotional home after so many years alone swept across his heart.

He felt the change in Bailey's body the instant it began. He gave her precisely what she needed, catapulting them both into a kaleidoscopic world of sensory pleasure as their bodies detonated simultaneously.

They collapsed in the aftermath of the sensual storm that overtook them, clinging tightly to each other as their bodies slowly relaxed and their respiration returned to normal.

Patrick held Bailey as her body went slack and she drifted into a peaceful doze. Although exhausted, he didn't sleep for a very long time. His mind wandered as he reflected on what they'd just shared and speculated on what they faced once this night ended. He knew that confrontation lay ahead of them. He told himself that he was prepared for it, but he wondered if he was.

He needed to believe that Bailey could embrace the future with him. As much as he wanted her, he feared that he was being overly optimistic. Whatever happened, he vowed yet again not to give up on her. He loved her, and he wasn't willing to allow her to be guided by fear or any other negative emotion.

EIGHT

Late for a breakfast meeting, Bailey placed a hastily written note for Patrick next to the coffeemaker, then grabbed her purse and a folder of job-site specs from the kitchen counter. She was relieved that he was still asleep, because she wasn't ready for the discussion they needed to have. *Coward*, her conscience chirped.

"Leaving already?"

Patrick stood in the entryway to the kitchen, leaning against the door frame, arms crossed over his chest and a somewhat subdued expression on his face.

She smiled wanly. "Good morning. I thought you were still asleep."

"Not anymore."

Clad only in a towel knotted low on his hips, he might as well have been naked. Bailey felt her senses leap into overdrive as she scanned his powerful body. More appealing and desirable than any man she'd ever known, he reminded her of a walking advertisement for sensuality. The urge to touch and be touched burst to life within her, and it was all she could do to restrain herself.

"Early meeting?" he asked.

She nodded, not at all reassured by his even tone. "It's a breakfast meeting with the Water Resources Board." Bailey glanced at her watch. "I'm late as it is. The coffee's still hot, and there's fresh pastry from Antoine's in the bread drawer."

"You're forgetting something."

Her smile disappeared. She knew she'd never forget anything connected to this man. "I don't think so."

"What about the promise you made to me at three o'clock this morning?"

"It's a promise I intend to keep, Patrick."

"Then we'll talk tonight?"

"Tonight," she confirmed. "I don't enjoy being a coward."

He frowned. "You're not a coward, Bailey."

"At the very least I've been behaving like a total wuss, and we both know it."

"Hardly."

"Then what am I?"

"The woman I . . ." He paused, then exhaled audibly. "You're the woman I want, Bailey Kincaid."

Why, and for how long? she couldn't help wondering. She searched his features, but his expression remained too enigmatic to read.

"How about seven o'clock in my suite at the Biltmore?" he asked.

She nodded. "Why don't I stop at Double Happiness Restaurant on my way to the hotel?" She wanted their conversation to be private, not conducted in a place crowded with strangers. "Would you like something special, or are you willing to trust me with our menu?"

"I trust you, Bailey, even when I don't like some of the choices you make."

She knew what he meant, so faulting him wouldn't be fair. She'd been running and hiding for years now, she realized, and Patrick hadn't let up on her until she'd faced that grim fact. But what would she do? She honestly didn't know.

He extended his hand. "Come here, love."

Bailey sensed he needed additional reassurance that she intended to keep their date. Despite his strong personality, he possessed a vulnerable side that he'd allowed her to see since his arrival in Santa Barbara. She had also witnessed his innate decency and consideration for others. She knew that those qualities were just a few of the many facets to his unique character that she'd blinded herself to in the past.

"Meet me halfway," she suggested, certain that he would grasp her true meaning.

He gazed at her for several quiet moments, a

thoughtful expression on his face. "Always, Bailey. Always. You have my word on it."

Relief crashed over her like a heavy, storm-induced surf. She released the breath she'd been holding. Leaving her things on the kitchen counter, she took a step in his direction. And then another. He matched her footstep for footstep until they met in the center of the kitchen.

She asked, "Now what?"

"Now we put our arms around each other."

"I can do that," she whispered, an array of emotions threatening to swamp her.

He slid his palms up the length of her arms to her shoulders and then gently drew her close. She felt the fierce pounding of his heart against her breasts and the furnacelike heat emanating from him as she sank against his muscular, hair-roughened body. Her heartbeat thundered in her ears, and she shivered when he pressed a kiss to the side of her neck.

Bailey forgot about being late for her meeting. She forgot everything in the moments that followed, everything but the man who held her with such remarkable gentleness. She needed every possible second with Patrick.

His lips moved up the side of her neck, along the curve of her jaw, and then settled over her mouth. He tasted of mint-flavored toothpaste and heated desire.

Slipping her arms around his waist, Bailey savored the flavors of his passion. She marveled over the remarkable sense of completeness she experienced every time he embraced her. No man had ever touched her heart and soul with such a devastatingly thorough impact. She doubted that any other man ever would. But was she strong enough to take the risks that accompanied the emotions she felt?

Desire flared deep inside her, bursting into flames and sweeping over and through her until she felt in danger of being consumed. After the night they'd shared, she couldn't believe how much she wanted Patrick again.

Bailey's pager, attached as always to the waistband of her jumpsuit, vibrated. She jumped, then groaned her annoyance at the interruption.

Patrick released her lips and peered down at her. "The world's intruding on us again."

"It's probably Jack Martin, one of the people I'm supposed to be meeting this morning." She unhooked the pager and studied the digital message before glancing up at Patrick. "Sure enough, it's Jack, and he's not known for his patience."

He kissed her forehead. "Go ahead, love. I've got to dress and be on my way too."

She stroked his hard cheek with her fingertips, her gaze sweeping over his face as she memorized his features once again.

He covered her hand with his and brought her fingertips to his lips. He pressed a kiss to the tips of her fingers, turned away from her with obvious reluctance, and strolled out of the kitchen with the innate confidence of a man who routinely conquered the world.

A melancholy smile on her face, Bailey watched him until he disappeared into her bedroom. She reclaimed her purse and the file folder she'd abandoned on the kitchen counter.

Making a beeline across the patio to her office in the main house, she placed a call to Jack Martin and then waited nearly ten minutes before the connection was made by the mobil operator. He informed her that their meeting location had been changed to a prospective building site, rather than in the suite of offices the Water Resources Board occupied in downtown Santa Barbara.

As one of several independent geologists who advised the board, she had to attend the meeting. She spent another five minutes looking for her copy of a document that Jack wanted her to bring.

Intent on quickly reaching her destination, she hurried out to the garage, climbed into her Jeep, and started the engine. Patrick's limo pulled up at the curb in front of the house just as she backed out of the long driveway. She waved at the driver, then accelerated down the street.

At first Bailey didn't even notice the black, low-slung European sports car that followed her as she drove the roads that wound their way east of the beachfront community. As traffic thinned, however, she picked up on the driver's aggressive nature as he hugged her rear fender and revved his engine.

Bailey refused to speed up. She knew the dangers of the narrow roads that laced the foothills of the mountains, so she eased her Jeep onto the shoulder once it was safe to do so, waved the unknown driver on, and then resumed driving. Her thoughts turned to Patrick once the sports car shot out ahead of her and roared around a curve in the road.

She no longer doubted that Patrick was the kind of man capable of sharing his strength with her. He'd repeatedly demonstrated that ability.

Their relationship was not some shallow exercise devoted solely to sexual gratification. But what exactly was it? Did they both have their emotions on the line, or was she the only one falling in love?

Passion was an integral element of it, given their intense attraction to each other, but she knew that there had to be more depth and texture to a relationship, or it would fail. She wanted everything a woman could want with a man. But what did *he* want?

As a lover, Patrick embodied every fantasy she'd ever had. As a man, he possessed integrity and a conscience. But would his heart remain guarded? His dating history suggested that he favored long-term affairs and nothing more. Bailey realized that until she clearly understood his agenda, there was no way she could reveal her deep feelings for him.

Patrick Sutton, she decided, had some explaining of his own to do. She knew she needed to overcome a lot of anxiety and self-doubt, but their discussion that night would have to be fair and equal. Otherwise, she didn't plan on saying a whole lot.

Why court rejection? she asked herself. Why, indeed?

As the road grew increasingly more narrow and twisting, Bailey focused her attention on her driving. She downshifted for the hairpin curve fifty yards ahead, but not quickly enough to avoid the car that suddenly darted out of nowhere and then stopped in the center of the road.

In the next second she recognized the vehicle as the one that had passed her a short while earlier. She simultaneously wrenched the steering wheel to the left and slammed on her brakes to avoid broadsiding the car.

Bailey heard her tires screech in protest as the Jeep lost traction on the mist-dampened cement. She felt the skid as soon as it began. She fought it, but her efforts proved futile. She careened off the road, a steep hill looming in front of her. Below the hill was a thirty-foot-deep ravine that she and Jeff had explored as children.

Bailey screamed as the Jeep lurched violently over the rutted terrain of the narrow shoulder of the road, crashed down the hill, flattening small trees and shrubs along the way, and then went flying into midair. Because she'd neglected to fasten her seat belt, she went flying, as well, just a second before the Jeep slammed into a cluster of towering fir trees.

Bailey hit the ground hard, like a rag doll carelessly tossed aside by an angry child. She cartwheeled down the hillside, her momentum halted abruptly by several tenacious shrubs clinging to the rocky soil on the rim overlooking the ravine.

A moment before she lost consciousness, she smelled gasoline, heard a deafening explosion, and whispered Patrick's name.

Patrick glanced up from the paperwork he was reading when his driver slowed the limo and came to a stop on the shoulder of the road. "Something just exploded on the far side of the hill, Mr. Sutton. I'm going to see if there's been an accident or if anyone needs assistance, so please remain in the limo, sir."

Patrick's first impulse was to ignore the driver's instructions, but he'd promised Francesca Reed that he would cooperate with her people for the sake of his own safety, so he remained in the vehicle.

He scanned the road ahead, registering the presence of another car, brake lights glowing, less than fifty yards away. He frowned as he glanced at the license plate. The driver of the European import suddenly sped off, tires squealing and rubber burning a black streak into the pavement.

A sense of unease claimed Patrick. It was compounded by his driver's stricken facial expression as the man jogged back to the limo. He thought of

Bailey, but he told himself that he had to be wrong. His gut told him something else altogether, though. He knew then that something had happened to her. Something very bad.

"It looks like Miss Kincaid's Jeep, sir, but I—"

Before the limo driver could finish his sentence, Patrick bolted out of the limo and ran to the edge of the road. When he saw the burning Jeep, his heart froze in his chest for what seemed like an eternity.

"Call 911!" he shouted over his shoulder as he raced down the steep hill.

Another explosion rocked the hillside. Patrick fell to his knees, righted himself, and continued on, crashing through the foliage that cluttered the rugged terrain. "Bailey! Answer me, damm it! Bailey!"

He finally reached the vehicle. Circling the burning wreckage, he saw no sign of her. The stench of burning metal and fuel invaded his senses as he searched in vain.

He stood as close as he could to the Jeep, watching helplessly. Dense smoke billowed around him. Tears of anguish streaked his face. Patrick didn't notice the limo driver until the man joined him.

"Sir, it's not safe for you to be out in the open."

Patrick gave the man a blank look. It took a moment for his meaning to register. "It doesn't matter anymore."

Sirens screamed in the distance. Patrick refused to leave Bailey to the care of strangers. He maintained a vigil near the Jeep, damning both fate and his own stupidity. He'd never told Bailey how much he loved her.

Emergency vehicles, fire trucks, and police units converged on the scene. In the controlled chaos that ensued, they extinguished the fire in the Jeep and then doused the surrounding landscape with hundreds of gallons of water to prevent any subsequent fire danger to the hillside.

Patrick joined the police officers combing the area on the off chance that Bailey hadn't used her seat belt and had been thrown free of the Jeep. The search proved fruitless, however.

When one of the fireman suggested that he return to the limo until the police could take his statement, Patrick ignored the man and continued to search for Bailey, even though his common sense told him he was wasting his time. The sound he heard a couple of minutes later brought him up short.

At first he thought he was imagining what he longed to hear, but then he realized that the moaning was real. Pushing his way through the thickets, he searched desperately for the source of the sound.

Patrick found Bailey sprawled on her back under a grouping of densely packed shrubs. Dropping to his knees beside her, he reached out, but he stopped himself when he realized that he might worsen her injuries if he drew her into his arms and held her. Instead of indulging the impulse, he clasped her hand between his own, thanked God that she was still breathing, and then shouted for help.

He rode with her in the ambulance as she drifted in and out of consciousness, unwilling and unable to ease his grip on her hand until one of the paramedics lost his temper and told him he might be endangering Bailey's life. Chastened, Patrick watched, stone-faced and numb inside, as they worked over her.

In the emergency room he refused to wait in the lobby. The implacable expression on his face was enough to persuade the doctors and nurses to allow him to remain at Bailey's side.

She regained consciousness, recognized him, and mouthed his name before a nurse placed an oxygen mask over her face. His self-control almost snapped as he watched her and listened to her struggle to breathe. She looked too fragile for words, and she'd nearly died.

Patrick left her side when he grew exasperated with the medical personnel caring for her. He grabbed the attending physician by the arm and hustled him into the corridor outside Bailey's examination room. "I want an MRI done on her now."

"It's premature," the doctor assured him.

"I'm only going to say this once, Doctor. I will put up the money for a new wing in this hospital before the end of business today, but only if you do precisely what I'm asking you to do."

"You aren't asking, Mr. Sutton. You're trying to

blackmail me into doing your bidding. We have the same agenda right now," he reminded him, "but there are medical procedures to be followed."

"This isn't a debate, Doctor, and I don't care whose rules you have to bend or break," he ground out. "I want an MRI done on her, and I want it done immediately. I won't have even the slightest injury to Miss Kincaid overlooked, or I'll deal with this institution legally. Are we clear?"

"You don't want to make threats against anyone when a police officer is nearby, Sutton." The speaker's voice was mild, but his message was clear.

Eyes narrowed, Patrick swung around and confronted Jeff Kincaid. "I'll do whatever it takes. Bailey's recovery is all I care about right now."

Jeff glanced at the physician. "Forget this conversation ever took place. Just take care of my sister." As the doctor returned to his patient Jeff studied Patrick, then nodded in the direction of an unoccupied examination room. "Let's take a break. You look like you need one, and I want to know how you happened to trip over the accident."

Patrick hesitated, his facial features like carved granite as he regarded Bailey's brother.

Jeff spoke quietly. "She's in excellent hands, so relax. I'd be in there with her if I thought differently. This is the same hospital where she had her appendix taken out when she was thirteen, where they reset and cast her broken arm when she was sixteen, and handled a sprained ankle she suffered during a marathon a couple of years ago. They really do know what they're doing, Sutton."

Patrick finally relented. He preceded Jeff into the examination room. Jeff closed the door.

"She's going to make it," Patrick told him, his voice ragged, his body so tense that every muscle ached.

"You might consider believing your own words."

Patrick jerked a nod in his direction, then walked to the window. His emotions started to unravel again as he stood there. He pinched the bridge of his nose with his fingertips, the stress of the last hour hitting him hard. He dragged in and then released one shuddering breath after another, struggling to master his emotions. It took him a few minutes, but he finally regained his composure.

"You're in love with her, aren't you?" Jeff asked.

"Yes," Patrick answered, his voice subdued.

"I thought so."

Patrick squared his shoulders, then turned to face Jeff Kincaid. "Do you have a problem with my feelings for your sister?"

"No, but she might."

"We're still trying to work our way through some of the debris from her past. At least we were until this happened."

Jeff studied him. "Sounds like we're on the same page. I don't want her hurt, Sutton. She took some knockout punches a few years back, courtesy of Jeremy Strong and his crowd. From what I can tell, you were, and still are, a part of that crazy world."

Patrick stabbed him with a hard look. "I'm one man, and I don't run with the pack. I'm not planning on changing my style anytime soon."

Looking satisfied with his response, Jeff nodded. "I guess I just wanted to hear you say the words."

Patrick relaxed a notch or two. "I can't believe this has happened."

"Bailey is generally a good driver. According to preliminary reports from the officers at the scene, the skid marks from her tires suggest that she was trying to avoid a collison with another vehicle. There were other skid marks, and they looked fresh."

Patrick nodded absently, not really hearing Jeff. His thoughts were on Bailey and his concern for her. He didn't like being away from her, even for a few minutes.

"Sutton?"

"Sorry."

"Baby sister won't approve if you cave in on her," Jeff cautioned.

Patrick chuckled, but his humor faded quickly. "Your sister is the feistiest woman I've ever known."

"I suspect that characteristic is part of her appeal for you. You're both strong people. Ought to make for some pretty interesting . . . discussions."

Both men turned when a knock sounded on the examination-room door. Patrick stiffened as it swung open.

A no-nonsense-looking nurse stood in the doorway. "Miss Kincaid is more alert now, although she's still taking oxygen. You've got five minutes with her before we take her upstairs for a CAT scan."

Patrick strode across the room before the woman finished speaking. Jeff followed. Patrick noticed the police officer stationed in the hallway before he walked into Bailey's room. Jeff's decision, he concluded, although he wasn't certain why. He planned to find out, though.

Half reclining against a mound of pillows and swathed in a crisp white sheet, Bailey appeared lucid. Patrick took in the abrasions on her forehead, cheeks, and shoulders, the fresh gauze dressing that covered the lower half of her left arm, and the fact that she was self-administering oxygen from a mask when she needed it.

He felt as if he'd been gut-punched. He fervently wished that he'd been the one hurt in the accident. He vowed then and there that he would do everything in his power to protect her in the future.

She coughed shallowly, then croaked, "Nothing seems broken, but I still feel kind of dented and a lot bruised."

Jeff shook his head, then leaned down to give her a brotherly peck on the portion of her cheek not daubed with antiseptic. "What the hell are we going to do with you?"

"Stay out of the hot tub. It's mine for the next month," she whispered, then took several deep breaths of oxygen before she met Patrick's gaze. "Hi there."

Heart lodged in his throat, Patrick took her hand. "Hi there, yourself."

Jeff announced, "I need to make a call. Why don't you two amuse yourselves for a minute?"

Neither Bailey nor Patrick acknowledged his comments or noticed his departure.

"Can I have a rain check?" she asked.

"For what?"

"Tonight."

He smiled at her, relieved that she had some of her old spirit back. "Of course."

Unable to stop himself, he leaned down and gently kissed her. She surprised him as she angled her head and parted her lips. He felt engulfed by her unexpected passion. Relief that she was alive and love for her detonated like a grenade inside him. He forced himself to end the kiss, though, because he knew she needed to rest.

"Did Jeff call you?"

"You don't remember?" he asked, his worry for her spiking again.

Coughing, she shook her head.

"I found you after your Jeep went off the road and the gas tank blew up."

"What happened?" She sighed, the sound leaden with fatigue. "I don't remember anything."

"Do you want me to tell Jeff?"

"Tell Jeff what?" asked her brother as he slipped back into the room.

Bailey's eyes fluttered closed. "I'm tired," she mumbled hoarsely, although her hold on Patrick's hand remained firm.

"She doesn't remember the accident," Patrick said, glancing at her brother.

Thanks to his recent experience with Tommy Dunlap, Patrick knew the dangers of head injuries.

"I'm not surprised," Jeff remarked. "She apparently bounced halfway down that hill."

An orderly pushing a gurney appeared in the doorway. Patrick stepped aside and watched as the man and the nurse who'd summoned them a few minutes earlier shifted Bailey onto the conveyance and wheeled her out of the room. She looked vulnerable and pale as she disappeared down the long hospital corridor.

He squared his shoulders and said the last thing he'd ever expected to say. "I have a terrible feeling that my executive assistant, Jeanne Carson, may have had something to do with Bailey's accident. I caught a glimpse of the license plate before the driver took off, and the car looked too familiar for it to have been a coincidence."

Jeff Kincaid peered back at him, his expression

cool, even detached. "That's quite an indictment. Care to tell me what went down?"

Patrick nodded. As if by agreement, the two men walked along the hallway as they talked.

"We left Bailey's cottage within minutes of each other this morning. I wanted to stop at the Fox Ridge property before going back to the Biltmore to get ready for a meeting this afternoon, so I had my driver take me there. We happened upon the accident just a moment or two after the Jeep exploded the first time. My driver—"

"One of Frannie's people?" Jeff asked.

Patrick met his gaze. "That's right. The driver pulled over to see if anyone needed help, but he asked me to remain in the limo for security reasons."

"That's his job, Sutton, so don't beat yourself up over it."

"I noticed a car on the road ahead of us a few seconds or so before the driver took off, but something about the license plate set off an alarm bell in my head."

"Jeanne Carson's license plate?"

Patrick nodded. "I think so, Jeff, although I can't be a hundred percent certain. That was when the limo driver thought he recognized Bailey's Jeep and ran back to the car to tell me what he'd seen. While he called 911 I went down the hillside to try to help her, but the Jeep was engulfed in flames and exploded a second time."

"You thought she was dead," Jeff said somberly.

"You're damn right I thought she was dead," he exploded, then took himself in hand and lowered his voice, "even though I didn't want to believe it. The emergency people showed up, and there was still no sign of her. Everyone hoped she'd been thrown clear, but no one knew for sure, so we kept looking. I heard her moaning and finally located her."

"Thank God for small favors," Jeff said, his tone far less detached. "There's something you need to know. Francesca called me just after I was notified about Bailey's accident. Before I had a chance to tell her what had happened, she voiced her concern about Ms. Carson."

"Does she have any evidence?" Patrick asked, still grappling with the shock that someone he'd trusted for the last fifteen years might have been responsible for Bailey's accident. And God only knew what else, he suddenly realized as he mentally ran down the list of incidents that had taken place during the previous six months.

"Francesca didn't say much. She's always been pretty closemouthed about her clients' affairs. Since she's new to your case, she's had to pull out all the stops. Unfortunately, her timing was off by a few hours. If Francesca is running true to form, my guess is that she's built a file on Ms. Carson that will amaze and horrify you, and it will absolutely thrill the district attorney. She's on her way up here to speak with us both and to see Bailey. She asked me to remind you that your personal safety is still an issue."

Patrick's temper flared. "I don't care about—"

"The woman you claim to love would care, Sutton. Although she hasn't ever discussed your relationship with me, I'm not blind. You're important to her, or you wouldn't be in her bed," he said bluntly. "Look, I don't want to see her life destroyed a second time because you used lousy judgment. You don't want that, either."

"You don't pull any punches, do you?" Patrick observed, his respect for Bailey's brother climbing several notches.

"Never, and I have it on good authority that that particular habit causes as many problems as it solves."

Patrick didn't miss his dry tone, and he couldn't help wondering about the link between Jeff Kincaid and Francesca Reed. When there was time, he planned to ask Bailey. He exhaled a hard gust of air, amazed by the turns his life had taken. "You and I are going to get along fine, I suspect."

Jeff gave him a curious look. "Why do say that?"

"We have a lot in common," Patrick answered.

Jeff laughed. "Poor Bailey. No wonder she's been so on edge the last several weeks."

Patrick spoke with renewed confidence, the kind of confidence intrinsic to his personality. "She'll be a hell of a lot calmer in the near future. I intend to make very sure of it."

The two men walked through the arched entry-way of a sparsely filled waiting room adjacent to the emergency room. As they strolled in the direction of an unoccupied grouping of chairs, Patrick felt the vibration of his pager. Only a handful of people knew the number, Jeanne Carson among them.

He paused. Jeff, still walking alongside him, stopped and glanced his way.

"What's up?"

"My pager," Patrick answered as he freed the device from his belt and read the digital message. He swore, the word utterly vicious, then got himself under control.

"What?" Jeff demanded.

"According to this, there's a message on my voice mail from Jeanne."

"Sounds like business as usual," Jeff observed. "Very clever, especially if she was involved in the accident this morning."

"Nothing gets in the way of Jeanne's dedication. Nothing."

The two men walked outside. Using the phone in the limo, Patrick checked his voice mail, which contained a reminder from Jeanne that she would be faxing material to him at his suite at the Biltmore for his afternoon meeting. He started to dial another phone number.

Jeff placed a hand on his arm. "Stay cool. You don't want to spook her now."

Patrick finished punching out the digits for Jeanne's direct line at the Sutton Group office in

Beverly Hills. He left a simple message in a voice filled with cold fury. "This is Patrick. I need you with me this afternoon."

"Think she'll show?" Jeff asked.

Patrick nodded as he handed the phone to the limo driver. "Absolutely."

"Why?"

"Several reasons, now that my brain's working again. First, she thrives on having an inside track on the make-or-break career deals the agency puts together. Second, she recently told me she'd do anything she had to do in order to protect my interests. Anything!" Patrick started walking again, his frustration with himself evinced by his inability to stay in one spot for more than a few minutes. "And since her divorce ten years ago, she hasn't had any kind of a life outside of her work. *Nada!*"

Jeff kept pace with him as Patrick paced one lane after another in the parking lot. "You couldn't have known what she was planning to do," he reminded him a few minutes later.

"I keep telling myself I have to be wrong, but I don't think I am. I just wish to God I'd seen the evidence, especially since it was right in front of me the entire time."

Jeff grabbed Patrick's arm. "What evidence?" he demanded.

Patrick jerked free of his restraining hand, but he didn't start walking again. "Everyone else at the office was victimized in one way or another, but never Jeanne. When I complained recently that I was fed up with one of my clients during the preliminary filming of a documentary, he almost died."

"Tommy Dunlap?"

He nodded. "In the aftermath of every single incident, Jeanne was on hand to tidy up the messes or to offer comfort, but she was never a target. Not once."

"Then it's time to devise an effective game plan," Jeff observed.

"The game is about to end." Patrick already knew what needed to be done. If Jeanne Carson was, in fact, the stalker, then he planned to be the person who took her down.

NINE

Jeff returned to police headquarters to assemble his surveillance team prior to Jeanne Carson's anticipated arrival at the Biltmore Hotel. Patrick devoted his energy to tracking down the neurosurgeon who was supposed to evaluate Bailey's CAT scan.

He wound up cooling his heels for more than an hour in the doctor's waiting room. His patience was stretched to the point of snapping by the time the doctor completed his surgery rounds and then read and interpreted the X-ray series done on Bailey.

Patrick learned that she hadn't sustained any neurological damage and that her memory loss wasn't uncommon, since she'd suffered a mild concussion. The doctor, who thought it best to admit her to the hospital for a twenty-four-hour observation period, indicated that she would probably remember the accident in fragments. After arranging for Bailey to be taken to a private room, Patrick informed Jeff of the test results and her room number at the hospital.

Patrick stopped in to see Bailey, but he didn't wake her. He sat in a chair beside her bed, oblivious to everything and everyone as he held her hand and watched her sleep.

He loved her, loved her more deeply than he'd ever thought himself capable of loving another person. He promised himself that he would express his feelings to her before the day ended. He felt responsible for what had happened to her, and his guilt fueled his determination to take her out of harm's way by any means at his disposal.

Although reluctant to leave her bedside, Patrick knew he had no other choice. He departed the hospital following a brief chat with her nurse and a longer conversation with the female police officer Jeff had assigned for Bailey's protection.

He directed his driver to take him back to the Biltmore, where Jeff and several officers, some garbed in attire suitable for hotel employees and others assembling electronic equipment in the bedroom of his suite, awaited him.

Unaware that Patrick's meeting had been rescheduled, Jeanne Carson arrived fifteen minutes early. Jeff's personnel tracked her from the moment she handed her car keys to the valet at the entrance to the hotel lobby.

When she arrived at his suite, Patrick recognized her distinctive knock on the door. Two sharp raps, a pause, and then a final rap of her knuckles. The sound reminded him of gunshots.

"All set?" Jeff asked.

His tension mounting, Patrick nodded.

"The room is wired. We won't miss a word."

Patrick placed the voice-activated pocket tape recorder he always carried with him on the coffee table. "Insurance," he told Jeff.

Bailey's older brother smiled, but his expression contained little mirth. "Let me know if you ever decide to change careers. I'll put you to work." Without waiting for a reply, he ducked into the bedroom and pulled the door closed behind him.

Patrick took a moment to steady himself before his confrontation with Jeanne Carson. Pulling open the front door of the suite, he stepped aside and was immediately assailed by the heavy scent of her trademark floral perfume.

"You look exhausted." She frowned in obvious disapproval as she placed her purse and briefcase on the table for four in the living room of the suite. She shrugged out of her suit jacket and draped the linen fabric across the back of a chair, then reclaimed her briefcase. "I thought the whole point of spending time up here was to relax."

Patrick managed a tight smile. "I've had some late nights with a friend."

"Miss Hard Hat of Santa Barbara County?" she asked, not bothering to mask her sarcasm. "Isn't she a bit below your usual standards, Patrick?"

"She's always had high standards, Jeanne. I

thought you knew that, since she was once married to Jeremy Strong."

"So that's why she looked vaguely familiar."

He shrugged, trying to appear indifferent. "Probably."

"She's not really your type."

"What's my type, Jeanne?"

Aware that their every word was being recorded, Patrick gripped the file he held until his knuckles whitened. He reminded himself to remain calm as he waited for her answer, despite the other impulses seething within him.

"You've always needed someone who understands you and the business we're in."

"Someone like you?" he asked very quietly.

"Now, that's an interesting concept." As she spoke she settled her bulk onto the couch, positioned her briefcase on her lap, and then opened it.

"How about another thought?"

She gave him an innocent look. "What do you mean?"

"You've been working awfully hard lately. I was thinking you might need some vacation time."

Jeanne frowned. "No, thanks."

"Why not? Surely there's a man in your life who'd like your undivided attention."

"You're it, boss."

She might have meant her words to sound lighthearted, but to Patrick they sounded ominous. "You're wrong. I'm not the man in your life,

Jeanne. And I never will be." He spoke quietly, but very firmly.

She waved her hand in dismissal. "Of course you are. I've devoted myself exclusively to you and the Sutton Group, and for only one reason."

"And that is?" he asked, inviting her to finish.

"I care about you, Patrick."

"I've always considered us good friends."

"We're more than friends. We're partners, in the truest sense of the word. That bond can't be broken."

"Is our friendship the reason you might have pushed the boundaries a little?"

She reached into her briefcase, but she kept her eyes on him. "What kind of boundaries are you talking about?"

"I was thinking along the lines of manipulating situations or people if things didn't go quite the way you wanted them to."

She smiled, but her facial expression looked brittle. Flushing, she shrugged. "Can you give me a specific example of what you mean?"

He made himself take a seat in a chair a few feet from her. "I think you know what I'm talking about, Jeanne."

"You mean like computer viruses, physical assaults, and fires in parking garages? Things like that?"

Patrick nodded, too sick at heart to speak for a moment.

"Since you benefited from those little accidents

of fate, why dwell on them?" she asked, one hand still placed atop the contents of her briefcase.

"How did I benefit?"

"They helped you to have the one thing you've always wanted," she explained, as though reasoning with a child. "Maybe you should consider thanking the person responsible for them, instead of acting suspicious about that person's motives."

Her reasoning was distorted, but Patrick thought he understood her reference. "Someone was trying to help me make Santa Barbara a reality, instead of a dream? Is that what you're saying?"

"Why else would *someone* have done all those things? That person would do almost anything for you and Daniel. That person wants you both to be happy. Santa Barbara makes you happy."

"Why?" Her mention of his son infuriated him, but he controlled his anger and stayed on track. "I was happy until this morning, Jeanne."

Her smile disappeared. Her expression turned glacial. "I don't know what you mean."

Patrick exhaled, his insides churning with renewed rage at her disregard for Bailey's life. "Bailey Kincaid is in the hospital. She could have burned to death when her Jeep exploded." He forced the words out, despite the pain they produced.

"Did she have an accident?"

"You know she did," he said quietly.

"How would I know anything of the kind?" she asked. "I assume she drove recklessly and paid the price. It happens, Patrick, so get over it. Someone solved a problem for you. It's definitely time for another thank-you note." She giggled, the high-pitched sound startling as it spilled free of her.

Stunned, Patrick simply stared at her. Who *was* this woman? And when had she gone over the edge? Why hadn't he seen it until now?

Her giggles finally under control, she remarked, "You didn't really want her, Patrick. Women like Bailey Kincaid are insignificant. They aren't good for much of anything except sex. They have no staying power and no understanding of true loyalty."

"Unlike you?" he asked.

She jerked a nod in his direction. "Now you're thinking clearly, boss."

"And Tommy? Another good deed?"

"You said he was annoying you. I guess your guardian angel took care of that situation too."

Patrick knew then that he was dealing with a psychopath. "You're the only person I spoke to about the situation."

"Someone must have overheard us." After withdrawing her hand from her briefcase, she closed the leather container and set it to one side on the couch.

Patrick froze when he saw the small pistol gripped in Jeanne's right hand. He lifted his gaze from the weapon to her flushed facial features.

"Are you my guardian angel, Jeanne?"

"I've always been your guardian angel."

"Then I should be thanking you, shouldn't I?"

She nodded as she used her free hand to massage her shoulder. "I did . . . my best, Patrick. I've always . . . done my best . . . for you." Jeanne's shortness of breath made her sound as though she'd just completed a marathon.

Patrick remained calm. "Then you don't need that gun, do you?"

"You're . . . going . . . to tell . . . on me," she rasped out. Tears seeped from her eyes. "Aren't . . . you?"

"There's nothing to tell," he assured her, taking in the increasing redness of her face and the way in which she was rubbing her shoulder. "But what if someone connects you to the accidents?"

"Won't . . . happen." She gasped. The muzzle of the gun dipped and swayed in her shaking hand. Muttering angrily at herself, she gripped it more tightly.

Despite having a weapon pointed at him, Patrick continued to speak, but he kept his voice low and unthreatening. "You sound very sure of yourself."

"I am."

"There may have been witnesses."

She shook her head. "No. I'm . . . careful." She sucked in a harsh-sounding breath, and then a second one. "You'll . . . protect . . . me. I'm your . . . friend and . . . best ally."

You, lady, are my worst nightmare, Patrick thought.

He watched Jeanne claw suddenly at the top

button of her blouse. It popped off. Patrick surged to his feet, certain now that she was having a heart attack.

Jeanne heaved herself upward, swayed once she got to her feet, and then staggered a few steps forward. She still held the gun. "Air," she cried. "Need . . . air."

"Put the gun down, Jeanne."

Halfway to the patio doors, she grabbed the back of a chair to steady herself. "Can't," she insisted.

"You're having a heart attack, Jeanne. Put the gun down so that I can call for a doctor."

Still holding the weapon, Jeanne Carson dragged in a noisy breath, then lurched for the open patio doors. Patrick moved swiftly, but not swiftly enough.

Jeanne turned just as he came up behind her. With the pistol jammed against his ribs, he froze, his gaze riveted on the blotchy face and agony-filled eyes of the woman who'd tried to destroy his entire world.

"Jeanne . . ." he began, but he stopped when he realized that she was struggling to speak.

"I . . . love you, Patrick . . . I've always . . . loved you."

The gun thudded to the carpet a moment later. Before Patrick could react, Jeanne Carson clasped her chest with both hands and groaned. The pain of what appeared to be a heart attack drove her to her knees before she slumped to the floor.

Patrick reached for a nearby telephone, torn between his loathing for the acts she'd committed against so many innocent people and the very human impulse to summon help.

The bedroom door burst open. Jeff Kincaid and two uniformed officers rushed into the room. "Medical personnel are on their way."

Jeanne writhed on the carpet, clutching at her chest and gasping for air as two police officers dropped to their knees on either side of her and began to assist her. Turning away from the unfolding drama, Patrick walked out onto the patio of his suite and into the sunlight.

Deeply saddened by what he'd just experienced, he gripped the balcony railing, bowed his head, and said a prayer of thanks that Jeanne hadn't managed to kill anyone. Especially Bailey. He straightened a few minutes later when he felt a hand settle on his shoulder. Turning, he met Jeff Kincaid's compassionate gaze.

"Without your help, we wouldn't have nailed her."

"If it hadn't been for me, none of this would have happened in the first place."

"Not real productive thinking, buddy. Baby sister won't approve, so shift forward now and let go of this before it eats you alive. You can't change what's gone down."

"Will she live?"

"The paramedics don't look real optimistic, but

they're trying to stabilize her. She's had a major heart attack."

Patrick shook his head, disbelief and several other emotions jumbled up inside of him. "I'm going to tell Bailey about the situation tonight."

"Why don't you save it for another time?" Jeff suggested. "She needs a lot of rest and even more happiness."

Patrick's pager vibrated before he could say anything more. He freed the device and read aloud the digital message. "I have a craving for vanilla-fudge ice cream."

Jeff grinned. "Bailey's going to be just fine." Crossing the shallow balcony, he paused at the entrance to the suite. "This may be a tad premature, but welcome to the family."

Patrick stared after him as he left the suite. He wished he shared Jeff's optimism that Bailey was ready to stop wrestling with the demons from her past and embrace the future with him. Unfortunately, he didn't feel at all optimistic, but he refused to give up hope.

Patrick showered and dressed before speaking at length with Francesca Reed. He'd already concluded that Jeff's evaluation of her competence and Bailey's faith in her were wholly justified. He regretted not employing her sooner.

Francesca had uncovered evidence linking Jeanne to Tommy Dunlap's car wreck and subsequent life-and-death struggle in a Los Angeles hospital. She'd traced the sabotage at Fox Ridge to Jeanne, as well, by using sources in both law enforcement and the well-drilling community. She then provided a shocking portrait of psychological deterioration that tracked Jeanne's transition from devoted and trusted assistant to an unstable woman with an obsession. In her quest to attain her goals over the years, it was clear to Patrick that Jeanne Carson had victimized countless innocent people.

After thanking Francesca for her thoroughness and severing the phone connection, Patrick realized that it would take him time to come to terms with the events that had taken place. What stunned him the most as he pondered the information provided by Francesca was Jeanne's apparent belief that he would approve of her methods and support them. He felt a profound sense of sadness.

On the heels of that melancholy emotion, he began to feel renewed hope for a future with Bailey. If she would have him, he wanted her—now and forever. He wouldn't settle for anything less. He knew in his heart that he couldn't.

As for Jeanne Carson, he felt nothing but relief that she'd been stopped. In ICU now, Jeanne had only a slim chance for survival. Patrick had faith that the courts would effectively deal with her if she survived the heart attack. He intended to be on hand to see the legal process through to its natural conclusion.

Patrick made a concerted effort to set aside his

anger with Jeanne, because he didn't want it to taint his life. Revenge had never been one of his goals, and it wouldn't be now, he privately vowed. He simply wanted justice and safety for those he loved.

Patrick left the Biltmore Hotel as dusk settled over the beachfront community. His limo driver took him to the hospital. They made two stops on the way there. He dismissed the man for the night before entering the building and taking the elevator to Bailey's room.

A uniformed police woman stood at the entrance to the suitelike hospital room. After checking his identification, she stepped aside. Patrick paused in the doorway, taking in the vases of fresh-cut flowers that littered nearly every available surface in the room before his gaze settled on Bailey. She appeared to be asleep, so he quietly crossed the floor, stopped at her bedside, leaned down, and lightly kissed her lips.

As he straightened she opened her eyes. "Just the man I've been wanting to see," she murmured.

"Does that mean you missed me?" He handed her a bouquet of long-stemmed red roses as he spoke.

"They're beautiful," she said, bringing the blossoms to her face and breathing deeply of their scent. "And yes, I've missed you. Hospitals are pretty boring places."

"And they obviously don't have the right flavor of ice cream." He smiled as he pulled a pint of ice cream, napkins, and two plastic spoons from the paper bag he held.

She grinned. "We'll have to note that on the comment card when I check out of this establishment."

He chuckled as he popped the lid on the ice-cream container. After handing her a spoon and napkin, he took a seat in the chair beside her bed. "Dig in," he invited, amazed by her cheerfulness.

"You get a gold star for this, Mr. Sutton."

"I'd rather have a kiss."

"That can be arranged," she said shyly. She dug her spoon into the ice cream with almost childlike glee. After tasting it, she groaned her pleasure. "This stuff always makes me feel better."

"I thought that was my job."

"All right," she agreed.

Patrick laughed. "You're getting easy in your old age."

"Be nice. I can't defend myself right now."

He sobered instantly. "I almost lost you this morning."

"Well, you didn't, so don't borrow trouble. I'm doing a lot better, and I'm starting to remember bits and pieces of the accident," Bailey admitted.

"The neurosurgeon said it would be best to let you remember on your own, so I can't volunteer to fill in the blanks."

She helped herself to another spoonful of ice cream before she said anything more. "I assume he knows what he's talking about, so I bow to his expertise."

"What I can tell you is that the person who caused the accident has been identified and stopped."

"That's a relief." She sighed and sank back against the pillows.

Relieved that she didn't seem inclined to know the identity of the other driver, Patrick took her spoon and placed it and the pint of ice cream on the bedside table. "Tired, love?" he asked.

She nodded. "The fatigue hits me in waves. I'm good for about fifteen or twenty minutes, then I get a case of the yawns. I should apologize in advance, since I'll probably fall asleep in the middle of a sentence."

"I'm not going anywhere, Bailey."

She extended her hand to him. He clasped it firmly, his gaze scanning the scratches on her face and dark shadows beneath her large blue eyes.

She studied him with equal intensity. "You look worn-out, Patrick."

He glanced across the room at the couch and chairs. "I'll probably stretch out on the couch a little later."

"You should be in a proper bed," she chided.

"In a couple of nights, with you, if you'll have me," he said.

"I think we need to talk first, don't you?"

"I'm counting on it, but in the meantime I'm

not leaving this hospital until you're ready to check out."

"The doctor said in a few days, if everything goes as he expects tonight."

"Well, I'm here to help the process along."

"You already have," she assured him.

"How's that?"

"By being here with me."

He leaned forward, unable to resist the allure of her lips. He kissed her gently, savoring the taste of her as their tongues tangled. Passion flared between them, passion so intense that Patrick had to put the brakes on the feelings flooding his senses and igniting in his bloodstream. He reluctantly released her lips.

He saw the tears that welled in Bailey's eyes a few moments later. "You okay?" he asked, alarmed. "Are you hurting? Do you need the nurse?"

She shook her head and blinked away her tears. "Sorry. That keeps happening, and I don't seem to be able to stop it."

"You've had a hell of a tough day," he reminded her.

"Sure feels that way," she admitted. "I'm usually not such a big baby, though. If I'm not dozing off, I'm getting all teary-eyed. At this point I honestly don't know which is worse."

"I don't care if you turn into a waterfall."

She laughed. "You may get drenched a few more times, so find an umbrella," she teased. "The good news is that I don't snore."

"Are you sure about that?" he asked, her whimsical mood contagious.

Bailey frowned at him. "I do not snore, Mr. Sutton."

He smiled at her. "Whatever you say, Ms. Kincaid."

She sighed softly, and her eyes fell closed.

"I'll be here when you wake up."

"Promise?" she whispered without opening her eyes.

"I promise."

Patrick watched her drift off. He remained in the chair next to her bed, holding her hand while she slept for almost an hour. A nurse came in to check the monitors grouped around the head of her bed and take her blood pressure. Bailey didn't awaken thanks to the woman's light touch.

When she started mumbling in her sleep and shifting atop the mattress, Patrick spoke qentle reassuring words. Bailey quieted immediately, but he didn't release her hand.

When she finally opened her eyes, she seemed surprised to see him. "You're still here."

"I always will be, if you'll let me."

"Oh." Her smile faded, and a look of uncertainty replaced it. "Did I tell you before that Pete Higgins stopped in to see me before you arrived?"

Although disappointed by her nervous reaction, Patrick didn't press her. He shook his head in response to her question.

"Fox Ridge is ready for Charlie Cannon's people to get started on your house. You'll have a viable water source for your home by noon tomorrow."

"You must be very proud of your people," Patrick remarked.

"Extremely proud, but the security Frannie arranged really gave them the peace of mind to focus their attention on the job and not worry about someone trying to sabotage them."

"So our professional relationship is over."

Bailey nodded. "That's true."

"So what happens now?" he asked.

Bailey shrugged, then looked down at her hands and examined her fingernails. "I guess time will tell." She exhaled shallowly, then darted a quick glance at him. "I'm going to be fine, Patrick. You don't owe me anything, and I don't expect anything from you."

"You have to be all right. I'm depending on it."

"I will be." She continued her study of her unmanicured fingernails.

Patrick forced himself to sound calmer than he actually felt. "Look at me, Bailey."

She did as he asked, but Patrick saw her wariness and uncertainty. "As for owing and expectations, you don't owe me anything. I do have some expectations of you, though."

"Why don't you tell me what's going on with you? How was your day? You don't seem like your old self tonight."

"My day was lousy, thank you."

She paled.

"Would you like to know why?"

"If you feel like telling me."

"You almost died this morning. That pretty well set the tone for the rest of the day."

"I'm—" she began.

He cut in, "Let's move on to the subject of expectations, why don't we?"

"All right."

"I have a whole raft of them where you're concerned, but that isn't surprising since I'm in love with you."

She stared at him, her surprise evident.

"That's not something you wanted to hear, is it?"

She didn't answer him. Instead, she said, "Say that again, please."

"I'm in love with you."

"I don't know what to say."

"You don't have to say anything," he told her.

"You mean it, don't you?"

Patrick watched as she sank back against the pillows and brought her fingertips to her forehead. "Of course I mean it. I've only said those words to one other woman, and she was Daniel's mother."

As her fingers came into contact with an abraded area on her forehead, Bailey winced.

"Talk to me, Bailey."

"I still don't know what to say."

"You can't be that shocked. In fact, I thought my feelings for you were pretty obvious."

He saw genuine shock in her eyes, and he didn't understand why. As far as he could tell, he'd done everything but put up a neon sign in the center of town that spelled out, in very clear terms, that he'd fallen in love with her. He asked the one question he'd prayed that he wouldn't have to ask, but he knew he needed to face the truth, whatever it was. "You don't love me, do you?"

"That's not true," she hedged.

"You do love me?" he pressed, his flagging hope somewhat revitalized.

She took a shallow breath, and then another. "I love you with all my heart, Patrick Sutton."

It was his turn, he realized, to be shocked. "How long have you known?"

Bailey glanced past him, her gaze roving over the flower-filled vases on the coffee table in front of the couch.

"I'm not going to let up until you tell me, Bailey."

She looked at him. "A long time, all right? A very long time, even though I didn't realize what I was feeling at the time."

He knew she couldn't mean what she was implying, but he asked anyway. "You're talking about those years in Los Angeles when you were . . ."

"Yes," she whispered, her admission punctuated by a huge yawn. "Especially that last year . . . and in the years after I returned to Santa Barbara. I tried to forget you, but I never did."

"You know now that I was attracted to you in

those days, and I almost tried to track you down more times than I can count."

"Attracted?" she said, repeating his word.

"That was part of it," he freely confessed. "You were beautiful and kind then, and you're those things, and many others now. Some people might consider me flawed because I wanted a client's wife, but I don't really care what other people think. I never have."

She smiled. "I always wondered what you were thinking when I'd catch you watching me."

"Would you like to know now?"

She pursed her lips, then nodded. "I think I would."

"Jeremy Strong was a foolish man."

She smiled wryly. "I figured I was the only person who thought that about him."

"Hardly, but if it's any consolation, he's finally cleaned up his act."

"He needed to. And for his current wife's sake, I hope he continues to walk the straight and narrow."

"They're doing fine."

He looked at her for several long moments. She peered back at him. Then she started to smile.

"What's so funny?"

"You. Me. Us. Our situation. Life." She shrugged, soft laughter escaping her. "Pick one."

"I surprised you, didn't I?" he remarked.

"You stunned me," she corrected.

"I want us to share our lives, Bailey."

"We're dating. That's sharing." She smothered her next yawn with the palm of her hand. "Sorry."

"You're forgiven, but only if you say you'll marry me."

She snapped her mouth shut, stared at him for a full minute, and then asked, "What? Why?"

"I want you to marry me so that we can build a life together."

"We *are* together," she protested. "And it's too soon to talk about marriage, Patrick."

He disagreed. "It's never too soon when two people love each other."

She reached for his hand and gripped it tightly. Their palms mated, and their fingers tangled together in a loose weave. "I need to think about it, so for now will you just hold me, please? I need to feel your arms around me."

"I'm not letting you go," he cautioned, alert now to her talent for delaying tactics if she felt uneasy or didn't want to be pinned down. "And this conversation is far from over."

"I didn't ask you to let go," she pointed out. Leaning forward, she kissed him with a passion that belied her fatigued state. Once she drew back, she curved the palm of her hand against his cheek. "I do love you, Patrick. I can't imagine not loving you." With that, she settled back in her hospital bed.

He recognized the extent of her struggle to stay awake in the moments that followed. Acutely aware of what she'd gone through because of him, he decided not to press her any further.

Patrick got up from his chair and crossed the room. After speaking briefly with the officer stationed at the door, he closed it. He proceeded to extinguish all the lights in the room except for the softly glowing panel located behind the head of Bailey's hospital bed. He adjusted the panel to a lower wattage that wouldn't disturb her sleep.

Kicking off his shoes, he joined her, stretching out beside her atop the sheet that was drawn up to her waist. He gathered her into a gentle embrace, basking in the feel of her shapely body aligned to his and savoring the knowledge that she loved him. He felt strengthened by the fact that she had finally been able to move past many of the fears that were rooted in her past.

He heard her sigh as she turned in to him and slipped her arms around his neck. Bailey's breathing quickly deepened, and he realized that she'd fallen asleep again.

Although he'd kept the promise he'd made to himself earlier that day, Patrick believed that expressing their love for each other was only the first step in their shared destiny. He wanted a lifetime commitment from her, and he didn't plan to give up on her until he had it.

TEN

Bailey awakened shortly before dawn. Patrick still slept beside her. Feeling both the press of his sturdy chest against her cheek and the encompassing strength of his embrace, she smiled. More rested now and grateful that her head no longer ached, she felt secure in his love for her and at peace with her past.

Bailey drifted with her thoughts until she recalled their conversation of the night before. She replayed it in her mind as she listened to the sound of Patrick's steady heartbeat.

He'd shocked her when he'd told her he loved her. She'd shocked him right back, she realized, by admitting her feelings for him.

Bailey's smile widened, the joy she felt unlike anything she'd ever experienced. The certainty in Patrick's voice when he expressed his love for her had blasted away the final barrier surrounding her heart. She felt able to love him freely and without the fear of impending betrayal. She also felt ready to plan a real future with him.

Marriage. Since her divorce, the word had conjured up images of betrayal. But now altogether different images played through her mind. Images of Patrick making love to her. Images of an intimate wedding on the patio of the house where she'd grown up, surrounded by friends, family, and her late father's fragrant roses. Images of the two of them sharing confidences, laughter, and goals. And images of making babies that they would raise in a home filled with love.

She wondered then about Daniel's reaction to their relationship. She wanted his approval of their marriage, and she hoped that he would want to be a part of their happiness.

Although guilty of hedging when Patrick had proposed to her, she didn't regret her desire to ponder the possibilities and consequences. Bailey realized that there would be consequences in the form of adjusting to his world, but she knew she could do it. Not just for Patrick, but for herself, as well.

She no longer feared everything and everyone connected to Hollywood, although she possessed sufficient honesty to admit to herself that she would be cautious about those people she welcomed into their life. She looked forward to making new, happy memories with Patrick to replace the sad ones. She knew that good and bad existed everywhere, not just in the land of smoke and mirrors.

Until a few days ago fear had been her watchword and her guide. Now her love for Patrick and her self-confidence guided her. A man of integrity and honor and conscience, he had earned and was worthy of her trust and love. She felt, in turn, worthy of him, because she was ready to be his partner in every sense of the word.

Bailey sighed softly, the happiness she felt like an unanticipated gift. It was magical, but not an illusion. It was as solid, passionate, and reliable as the man who made her feel more cherished than she'd ever thought possible.

"You're awake."

When she heard the sound of Patrick's voice, Bailey eased back a few inches and looked up at him. "How did you know?"

"You're breathing changed a little while ago."

"Very observant," she said softly.

"I learned to be alert when Daniel was a baby. I never broke the habit, I guess."

"I'm not a baby," she reminded him.

He tugged her body even closer. "You're right, you're not."

She laughed, then sobered when she felt the strength of his desire pressing against her abdomen. Hunger sparked to life deep inside of her body. "Can we lock the door?"

"As much as I'd like to, I doubt the nursing staff would approve."

"Shucks."

"My sentiments exactly." He studied her, a thoughtful expression on his face. "Your headache's gone, isn't it?"

She nodded.

"Your eyes are clear too."

"Thank you, Dr. Sutton."

"They showed your pain, Bailey."

"All gone. Not to worry."

"I'll believe that when the bruises are gone and the scratches have healed. I'll always worry about you. It's part of loving you."

She circled his neck with her arms, then nudged his head closer with her fingertips. Fusing her lips to his, she indulged herself with a lingering and very thorough kiss. As she angled her head and parted her lips, she tasted Patrick's desire for her as he thrust his tongue into her mouth and used it like a seductive rapier to ravage her mouth and her senses.

By the time he relinquished her lips, she felt flushed and dizzy with need. "I want you," she murmured as she hugged him and buried her face in the muscular curve that joined his shoulder and neck. "So much."

He groaned, the sound rife with frustration. "After we blow this pop stand. I promise."

"I'm holding you to your promise."

"I'm counting on it," he said, his voice ragged

as she undulated against his body. He grabbed her hips to end the torture.

"I can't seem to help myself," Bailey confessed.

"I noticed."

"It's your fault."

"How do you figure that?"

"You turn me on," she confessed. "You always have."

He peered down at her. "Always?"

"Yes, and I used to feel terribly guilty about my reaction to you."

"You never acted like you wanted me."

"Of course not. It wouldn't have been right."

"I understand. That's what held me back too."

"I know you well enough now to realize that you mean that."

Patrick nodded. "And I meant it when I told you I'm in love with you. Just as I meant it when I proposed to you last night."

"What about Daniel?"

"My son will approve."

She smiled, amazed as always by his confidence in his own judgment. "You sound very sure."

"After you left Los Angeles, my then seventeen-year-old son told me I was a fool to let you get away."

Startled, Bailey said, "How could he have known that we were drawn to each other?"

"He didn't know, but the kid has great instincts about people. He knew you were special, which is why he never forgot you."

"He hasn't called me. Was he upset that we were seeing each other?"

"He's just finishing up his quarterly exams, and he told me, without an invitation to discuss the subject, that I'd be a fool to let you get away a second time."

"I think I'll buy him a crystal ball when he graduates. He'll make a fortune."

Patrick laughed. "My son is smart enought to recognize a good woman when he sees one. I like to think he takes after his father."

"Whoever he takes after, I'm definitely going to watch myself when he's around."

"Daniel wants brothers and sisters."

She came right back at him with the comment, "Then I guess we'll have to give him some."

His humor fleeing, Patrick cupped her face between his hands. "Does that mean what I think it means?"

"It means you might consider a second proposal."

"Will you marry me, Bailey Kincaid? Will you share yourself, your love, and your remarkable view of life with me? Will you be the mother of my children, and will you love me forever?"

Tears filled her eyes. "Yes, I will marry you, Patrick Sutton. And, yes, to everything else you just asked of me."

"What changed?" he managed as he drew her into his arms and held her more tightly than she'd ever been held before.

"I changed. I stopped being afraid, because of you."

Patrick kissed Bailey then with the kind of tenderness that spoke of his deep and abiding love and of his understanding of the difficult path she'd walked in order to embrace the future with him.

THE EDITORS' CORNER

How often do you read a really good book? We hope that with LOVESWEPT, you read four. Per month. This month we're taking you on a trip around the country with four delightful romances from some of our best authors. From love on the range to the streets of New York and Dallas and the heart of the South, you're off on a journey of the heart.

The first gem is Marcia Evanick's **SILVER IN THE MOONLIGHT**, LOVESWEPT #906. Dean Warren Katz had nothing but the best of intentions when he wrote to Katherine Silver regarding the welfare of her aunts. He was just being neighborly to the little old ladies whose house was ready to cave in. When Katherine arrived in Jasper, South Carolina, it didn't take a genius to see that her aunts were hale and hearty. Now if she could just get her hands around Mr. Katz's neck. But he tells her to look below the surface, at the furniture placed to hide cracks in the walls, the broken shutters, not to mention the crumbling foundation, well hidden by a generous array of bushes. Sharing coffee, conversation, and a whole lot more, Dean and Katherine launch a crusade to renovate the house. Marcia Evanick's latest book is rich with romance, and highly reminiscent of mint juleps, old porches, rocking chairs, and, of course, starry southern nights.

RaeAnne Thayne returns with **SWEET JUS-TICE**, LOVESWEPT #907. Somehow Nicholas Kincaid can't believe Ivy Parker when she says that he wouldn't even notice the 500 sheep she wants to raise on his land. Ivy's ranch is already dangerously close to bankruptcy, and without the fresh grass on Kincaid's land, she'll have to sell off part of the herd to buy food for the rest. Nick is her only hope, but all he wants is some peace and quiet. Lord knows he needs it—he's spent the past year trying the most-watched case since the O. J. Simpson trial. Nick's motto is Don't get involved, but when he learns how desperate Ivy's situation is, he relents. Now her problems are his as well, and suddenly, being neighbors isn't so bad. And as he watches Ivy stand her ground against the rumors and mysterious occurrences on the ranch, he realizes that in her he may have found the home he's never known. RaeAnne Thayne weaves a sensual and moving tale of passion and intrigue on the range.

Fayrene Preston tells us Kylie Damaron's story in **THE DAMARON MARK: THE LOVERS**, LOVESWEPT #908. Contrary to popular belief, you can go home again, and David Galado has done just that—much to Kylie's dismay. From the time she was a little girl, Kylie had depended on David to be her fierce protector from the dark shadows that had haunted her life. A chance encounter and misunderstandings had reduced them to mere acquaintances, a pretense that David had always tried to uphold. But when David learns of Kylie's new boyfriend, a man with dangerous connections, he can't stop himself from getting involved. Kylie's wondered a thousand times over about what would have happened if David had never left in the first place, and here's her chance to find out. But when an attempt on her life is made, will she allow herself to trust her heart and her future to a man she once thought she loved? Fayrene Preston answers that question when two lost souls throw fate to the wind and find solace in each other.

In **HOT PROPERTY,** LOVESWEPT #909, Karen Leabo pits a tough-talking detective against his awfully beautiful suspect. For Wendy Thayer, turning thirty is rough, but getting arrested on her birthday has got to take the cake. Despite all her objections to the contrary, Michael Taggart hauls Wendy into the station house on charges of transporting stolen goods. But the beautiful personal shopper insists that she and her favorite client are innocent of any wrongdoing. And once she's located Mr. Neff, she'll prove it, she promises. Wendy knows there's been a huge mistake, sweet Mr. Neff just couldn't be a criminal. But as Michael and Wendy search for the elusive old man, more clues keep popping up to incriminate Wendy. Michael has learned to distrust any woman who loves to spend money, never mind a woman who does it for a living. But when the odds are against them, will he gamble away his dreams for the chance to be with Wendy? In a delightful tale of passionate pursuit, Karen Leabo sends two unlikely lovers on a journey to discover their own unspoken longings.

Happy reading!

With warmest wishes,

Susann Brailey　　*Joy Abella*

Susann Brailey　　　　Joy Abella

Senior Editor　　　　　Administrative Editor

P.S. Look for these women's fiction titles coming in October! From *New York Times* bestselling author Iris Johansen comes **THE FACE OF DECEPTION**, the gripping story of a forensic sculptor who is hired to reconstruct a face from a skull—and is rewarded for her efforts with an odyssey of terror. In **MERELY MARRIED**, Patricia Coughlin presents a stunning love story set in Regency England, where a scandalous scheme backfires on a crafty rake who is determined to take himself off the marriage market. And from Ellen Fisher, an exciting new voice in historical romance, comes **THE LIGHT IN THE DARKNESS.** The last thing Edward Greyson expected was to be taken with Jennifer Leigh Chilton, who has transformed herself into the perfect light to shatter his darkness. Yet, until he can escape his troubled past, and the horrible secret that plagues his soul, he can never be free to love again. And immediately following this page, preview the Bantam women's fiction titles on sale in September.

For current information on Bantam's women's fiction, visit our website at the following address:
http://www.bdd.com/romance

Don't miss these extraordinary
novels from Bantam Books!

On sale in September:

*AND THEN
YOU DIE*

by Iris Johansen

*WRITTEN IN
THE STARS*

by Katherine O'Neal

*CHARMED AND
DANGEROUS*

by Jane Ashford

"Iris Johansen keeps the reader intrigued with complex characters and plenty of plot twists. The story moves so fast, you'll be reading the epilogue before you notice."—*People*

AND THEN YOU DIE

by *New York Times* bestselling author

Iris Johansen

Bess Grady had heard the unmistakable sound before. She knows what it means. But not even the eerie lament of the howling dogs can prepare her for what has taken place in the small village. The seasoned photojournalist had been sent there on an easy assignment, and now she has stumbled upon something she was never meant to see. Amid chaos and fear, she joins forces with an intimidating stranger, a man whose alliances are unclear but whose methods have a way of leaving bodies in his wake. For what she has witnessed is only the first stage in a plan of terror that may kill us all. And she has no choice but to stop it—or die trying. . . .

Holy Virgin, help them. Their immortal souls are writhing in Satan's fire.

Father Juan knelt at the altar, his gaze fixed desperately on the golden crucifix above him.

He had been in Tenajo for forty-four years and his flock had always listened before. Why would they not listen to him now in this supreme test?

He could hear them in the square outside the church, shouting, singing, laughing. He had gone out and told them they should be in their homes at this time of night, but it had done no good. They had only offered to share the evil with him.

He would not take it. He would stay inside the church.

And he would pray that Tenajo would survive.

"You slept well," Emily told Bess. "You look more rested."

"I'll be even more rested by the time we leave here." She met Emily's gaze. "I'm fine. So back off."

Emily smiled. "Eat your breakfast. Rico is already packing up the jeep."

"I'll go help him."

"It's going to be all right, isn't it? We're going to have a good time here."

"If you can keep yourself from—" Oh, what the hell. She wouldn't let this time be spoiled. "You bet. We're going to have a great time."

"And you're glad I came," Emily prompted.

"I'm glad you came."

Emily winked. "Gotcha."

Bess was still smiling as she reached the jeep.

"Ah, you're happy. You slept well?" Rico asked.

She nodded as she stowed her canvas camera case in the jeep. Her gaze went to the hills. "How long has it been since you've been in Tenajo?"

"Almost two years."

"That's a long time. Is your family still there?"

"Just my mother."

"Don't you miss her?"

"I talk to her on the phone every week." He frowned. "My brother and I are doing very well. We could give her a fine apartment in the city, but she would not come. She says it would not be home to her."

She had clearly struck a sore spot. "Evidently someone thinks Tenajo is a wonderful place or Condé Nast wouldn't have sent me."

"Maybe for those who don't have to live there. What does my mother have? Nothing. Not even a washing machine. The people live as they did fifty years ago." He violently slung the last bag into the jeep. "It is the priest's fault. Father Juan has convinced her the city is full of wickedness and greed and she should stay in Tenajo. Stupid old man. There's nothing wrong with having a few comforts."

He was hurting, Bess realized, and she didn't know what to say.

"Maybe I can persuade my mother to come back with me," Rico added.

"I hope so." The words sounded lame even to her. Great, Bess. She searched for some other way to help. "Would you like me to take her photograph? Maybe the two of you together?"

His face lit up. "That would be good. I've only a snapshot my brother took four years ago." He paused. "Maybe you could tell her how well I'm doing in Mexico City. How all the clients ask just for me?" He hurried on: "It would not be a lie. I'm very much in demand."

Her lips twitched. "I'm sure you are." She got into the jeep. "Particularly among the ladies."

He smiled boyishly. "Yes, the ladies are very kind to me. But it would be wiser not to mention that to my mother. She would not understand."

"I'll try to remember," she said solemnly.

"Ready?" Emily had walked to the jeep and was now handing Rico the box containing the cooking implements. "Let's go. With any luck we'll be in Tenajo by two and I'll be swinging in a hammock by four. I can't wait. I'm sure it's paradise on earth."

Tenajo was not paradise.

It was just a town baking in the afternoon sun. From the hilltop overlooking the town Bess could see a picturesque fountain in the center of the wide cobblestone plaza bordered on three sides by adobe buildings. At the far end of the plaza was a small church.

"Pretty, isn't it?" Emily stood up in the jeep. "Where's the local inn, Rico?"

He pointed at a street off the main thoroughfare. "It's very small but clean."

Emily sighed blissfully. "My hammock is almost in view, Bess."

"I doubt if you could nap with all that caterwauling," Bess said dryly. "You didn't mention the coyotes, Rico. I don't think that—" She stiffened. Oh, God, no. Not coyotes.

Dogs.

She had heard that sound before.

Those were dogs howling. Dozens of dogs. And their mournful wail was coming from the streets below her.

Bess started to shake.

"What is it?" Emily asked. "What's wrong?"

"Nothing." It couldn't be. It was her imagination. How many times had she awakened in the middle of the night to the howling of those phantom dogs?

"Don't tell me nothing. Are you sick?" Emily demanded.

It wasn't her imagination.

She moistened her lips. "It's crazy but— We have to hurry. *Hurry*, Rico."

Rico stomped on the accelerator, and the jeep careened down the road toward the village.

They didn't see the first body until they were inside the town.

He is her sworn enemy.
She is the prize he wants above all.

WRITTEN IN THE STARS

From the winner of the *Romantic Times* Award for
Best Sensual Historical Romance

Katherine O'Neal

"Katherine O'Neal continues to reign as the queen
of romantic adventure."—*Affaire de Coeur*

*Diana Sanbourne is faced with an impossible choice: ignore
her father's dying wish or seek out the one man who can
fulfill it. The one man she despises—Jack Rutherford.
Once, she had loved him, only to be betrayed, and she
vowed never again to fall under the power of his seductive
caress. Now he's a rogue hunter of ancient relics, with the
daring and instincts that could lead to the fabled treasure
her father asked her to find. Yet even as he joins her on her
quest—one that will lead from England's shadowy under-
world to a treacherous distant land—Diana must guard
not only her life but her heart. For Jack makes it clear he
intends to reclaim her for his own. And she is just as determined not to surrender.*

"So you want to find your father's bloody treasure, do
you, Diana?" This wasn't the voice she remembered.
It throbbed and seethed and demanded with all the
passion she'd set loose. It stirred her deeply, causing
her breath to come in wispy gasps. "His obsession

with that treasure has destroyed my family and, I suspect, caused his own death. Would you like to see what it did to *me*?"

He jerked his jacket open and flung it, in one furious motion, across the room. Then he savagely ripped his shirt off, buttons scattering against the wooden floor, and sent it flying in the jacket's wake. As he did, Diana saw the criss-crossing of scars beneath the thick, dark hair and bronze expanse of his chest. His arms, sleekly muscled, were similarly scarred. When he turned his back to her she saw the faded tracks left by the cat-o'-nine-tails.

"Now tell me," he spat out, facing her again. "If my jailers couldn't break me, what makes you think I'd bend to your will?"

Her eyes had been riveted by the scars. Rather than deform him, they lent him the rugged, dashing quality of a martyr stoically holding his tongue beneath the most unimaginable torture. It actually made him more attractive, gave his finely honed body a sense of reckless adventure and romantic mystique.

Dragging her gaze back to his face, she said, "Because you owe me."

"I owe *you*? I'm the one who spent two lousy years in that hell-hole, wanting to die. I'm the one who had to wake up in the middle of the night to the sound of a turning key, knowing they were coming again, and wondering if I could take it one more time. *I'm* the one who didn't get so much as a *visit* from the woman who just two nights before had sworn to love me no matter what— If anything, baby, you owe *me*!"

She felt the outrage burst in her like a broken dam. "You insufferable boor! You wrested that promise from me under the falsest of pretenses. How could you have done that? To betray me so miserably after I gave you something I'd given no other man. I made *love* with you. I trusted you, Jack, with everything I had. And after all that, you didn't even have the decency to trust me with the truth. *Damn* you for what you did to us. If you rot in hell you can't make up for a *minute* of it."

That was why she hated him. That's why she'd do anything to see him on his knees before her.

But he wasn't on his knees. He was looking at her through a narrow, bitter gaze that spoke of his own betrayal at her hands. Yet it was the shrewd gaze of a quick mind ticking off the possibilities.

Jack remained as he was, stubbornly silent. There were things he hadn't told her, things that would help explain his actions. But now wasn't the time. He'd be damned if he gave her the satisfaction.

Diana straightened her shoulders, as if pulling together what was left of her dignity. His glance dropped to the out-thrust swell of her breasts.

"Tell me," he said, hooking one thumb beneath her jaw and lifting it to study her face. "Have you been with another man since our last encounter?"

"That's none of your concern," she snapped, jerking her chin away from his hand.

"No, but it would make the payment all the sweeter."

She narrowed her eyes. "What do you mean?"

"You want something from me. You've made it clear you'll stop at nothing. Should I leave now, no doubt you'll hound me until I tell you what you want to know. I hate to think what lengths you'll go to next. So the prudent thing would be to give in to your demands and be done with you once and for all. But that brings up the question of payment. You wouldn't expect to get something for nothing. And my services don't come cheaply, as you may know."

"Mercenaries never do."

"So, logically speaking, what have you to offer me?"

"Money," she said, a little too quickly.

"Money is of no use to me now. You don't have enough to make it interesting."

"What then?"

"What, indeed? What could you possibly have that would be worth my time?"

He was looking her up and down. "*Two minutes* of your time."

"Two years and two minutes," he corrected.

"That's not my fault."

"I'm a bitter man, Diana. I'm not ashamed to admit it. I despise you and your family every bit as much as you scorn me, if not more. I see it in your eyes that you want me punished for my sins. Well, guess what? I want you chastened just as much. So I ask myself, what could you possibly give me that would make your flesh crawl to hand over? What," he asked idly, tracing the back of his finger in a path from her collarbone to the soft mound of her breast, "indeed?"

She slapped his hand away. "If you think I'll stand still and let you blackmail me this way, you're madder than I thought."

"Cheeky words, coming from a kidnapper. We might as well be honest. We loved each other once, or thought we did, but we're adversaries now. We don't trust each other, and we each feel we have good reason. So any personal appeal you might make to me is guaranteed to fall on deaf ears. I'm on to you now, and am not bloody likely to fall prey to your trap a second time. I don't give a damn if you find your father's precious treasure. But since you do, here are my terms. I'll give you the information you want and you give me what you've—*given no other man.*"

"Jane Ashford is an exceptional talent."—*Rendezvous*

CHARMED AND DANGEROUS

by Jane Ashford

Gavin Graham works alone, trusts no one, and never, ever gives his heart. But the spy may have met his match in an ex-governess. Laura Devane has been handpicked to fulfill an important mission: distracting him from the deceptive charms of a Russian countess. Once, years ago, she defiantly rejected his marriage proposal. Now she meets his cool mockery and sensual advances with a maddening self-possession. And she plunges headlong into a perilous investigation that leaves him fearing for her safety. Clearly the woman is a menace—to international peace and to his peace of mind. For Laura's passion for intrigue matches his own, and her touch leaves him stunningly aroused, tempting him to join her in a life of dangerous desires. . . .

"You are looking very lovely this evening," said Gavin as he led Laura onto the dance floor at the Austrian embassy ball.

Startled, Laura looked up at him. It was the first compliment he had ever offered her, and she didn't trust it for a moment.

"That gown is unusual. But then, your clothes are all quite elegant."

She gazed down at the folds of her ball gown, fashioned of a silk that shimmered between bronze and deep green, depending on the light. She had been exceedingly pleased with the fabric and design from the moment she saw them. Looking at the gown now, she was filled with suspicion.

Gavin grasped her waist, and they began to dance, falling naturally, once again, into rhythm with each other. It was a waltz. Of course it was a waltz, Laura thought. A country dance or quadrille would offer him less scope to unsettle her.

"You're not usually so silent," commented Gavin, turning her deftly at the end of the room.

The strength of his arm was palpable, and his hands—on her back and laced with hers—held an unnerving heat. He was a man who demanded notice. You couldn't ignore him, and it would always be a serious mistake to discount him. At the same time, he made it terribly difficult to keep one's wits about one. It was a devastating combination. "Your coat is very well cut," she managed.

His eyes flickered, and one corner of his mouth turned up for a moment. "Thank you," he answered.

Evening dress did particularly become him, Laura mused. And he wore it with unmatched ease. She felt a flutter in her midsection, and wondered if her dinner was about to disagree with her.

"Having established that we are both creditably dressed, perhaps we could move on to some other topic," he added.

Always mocking, Laura thought. Did he speak seriously to anyone? To Sophie Krelov, perhaps? "Is Lord Castlereagh here tonight?" she asked him. "I haven't yet seen him."

"I believe so." Gavin turned his head to search for the chief of the English delegation at the congress. "He had planned to be."

"He must be eager not to offend the Austrians." Laura was also scanning the huge room.

"Indeed?"

Laura looked up at his surprised tone.

"And why should he be?" inquired Gavin.

"I assume he wants their support against Russia's demands."

"Has the general been educating you?" he said, with predictable irony.

"The general shares the common opinion that women understand nothing about politics," she responded tartly. "I believe he would sooner explain such matters to his horse."

"Oh, I think he would speak to the dog first."

Laura stared up at him, not sure she had heard correctly. A spurt of laughter escaped her.

"Where do you get your information, then?" he added.

"I am quite capable of reading."

"Reading?"

For some reason, the way he said the word made Laura recall the very unpolitical things she had read in the earl's private library. She flushed deep scarlet.

"Newspapers?" continued Gavin, looking fascinated at the reaction his remark had produced.

Unable to speak, she nodded.

"Perhaps not only the English papers? You seem to have a talent for languages."

"I have been reading all the accounts of the congress that I can find," she answered, regaining some measure of composure. "Hard as it may be for you to believe, I am deeply interested in what is going on here."

"It isn't at all hard for me to believe." His tone left Laura wondering whether he meant his words as an insult.

"It is oppressively warm in here, isn't it?" he remarked. In the next moment, he had led her into a tiny alcove and opened one of the French doors.

Then they were somehow through it and on a flag-stone terrace that flanked the building. A large garden spread into darkness on their left. "There, that's better."

"Mr. Graham!" Laura struggled a little in his grasp. "Excuse me. I wish to go back in." It was quite unsuitable for them to be outside alone.

"But it is such a beautiful night," he argued, his arm adamant around her waist.

"On the contrary, it is quite chilly," she said, trying to step out of his grasp.

He swung her down two shallow steps into the garden. It was all Laura could do to keep her feet. Beyond the squares of light from the ballroom windows, the night was lit by a half moon, which turned the landscape into a maze of black and silver. Gavin swept her along to a row of shrubbery, inky masses against the stars, which Laura recognized only when their needles brushed her arm.

"Mr. Graham," she protested more loudly. "I ask you, as a gentleman, to—"

"You and the general make the same mistake in thinking I am a gentleman," he said. With a jerk, he pulled her tight against him, his lips capturing hers in a hard, inescapable kiss.

Laura stiffened in surprise and outrage. She pushed against his shoulders—with no effect. She wriggled and managed only to make herself even more conscious of the contours of his body melded to hers. She had never been in such intimate contact with anyone. One of his hands had slid well below her waist and was pressing her even closer. The muscles of his chest caressed her breasts in the most amazing way. And his lips moved confidently on hers, rousing sensations that she couldn't evade.

It was unthinkable. It was intolerable. It was

rather like some of the things she had read, Laura mused dizzily. One couldn't really understand, through mere words, how it felt, how one's whole being could suddenly turn traitor and melt like ice in a conflagration.

In the next instant, she was thrust away roughly and left swaying on her feet at arm's length.

"There," said Gavin unevenly.

Laura could see his face only dimly in the light from the distant windows. She thought for a moment that he looked almost shaken. But in the next, the sneering mockery was back.

"Was that what you wanted?" he said.

"I . . . ?"

"When you allowed me to bring you out here?"

"Allowed?"

"If the general suggested such a ploy, he is even denser than I realized."

"You practically dragged me out of the ballroom," Laura accused.

"Dragged? I think not." He said it in a caressing tone that made Laura's face go hot.

"You . . . you bastard."

"Tch. Is this language for a lady?"

Sweeping back her skirts, Laura kicked him in the shin. "Be thankful I am a lady," she said over her shoulder as she strode back toward the ball. "If I were not, that might have hurt a good deal more."

His derisive laughter followed her up the steps onto the terrace. Laura turned to glare at him, and he raised one finger in a lazy salute. Her fists clenched, and blood pounded through her temples. If she had had a pistol at that moment, she thought, she would have killed him.

On sale in October:

THE FACE OF DECEPTION
by *Iris Johansen*

MERELY MARRIED
by *Patricia Coughlin*

THE LIGHT IN THE DARKNESS
by *Ellen Fisher*

Bestselling Historical Women's Fiction

AMANDA QUICK

____28354-5 SEDUCTION . . .$6.50/$8.99 Canada

____28932-2 SCANDAL . . . .$6.50/$8.99

____28594-7 SURRENDER . . . .$6.50/$8.99

____29325-7 RENDEZVOUS . . . .$6.50/$8.99

____29315-X RECKLESS . . . .$6.50/$8.99

____29316-8 RAVISHED . . . .$6.50/$8.99

____29317-6 DANGEROUS . . . .$6.50/$8.99

____56506-0 DECEPTION . . . .$6.50/$8.99

____56153-7 DESIRE . . . .$6.50/$8.99

____56940-6 MISTRESS . . . .$6.50/$8.99

____57159-1 MYSTIQUE . . . .$6.50/$8.99

____57190-7 MISCHIEF . . . .$6.50/$8.99

____57407-8 AFFAIR . . . .$6.99/$8.99

IRIS JOHANSEN

____29871-2 LAST BRIDGE HOME . . .$5.50/$7.50

____29604-3 THE GOLDEN
                      BARBARIAN . . . .$6.99/$8.99

____29244-7 REAP THE WIND . . . . . .$5.99/$7.50

____29032-0 STORM WINDS . . . . $6.99/$8.99

Ask for these books at your local bookstore or use this page to order.

Please send me the books I have checked above. I am enclosing $____ (add $2.50 to cover postage and handling). Send check or money order, no cash or C.O.D.'s, please.

Name _____

Address _____

City/State/Zip _____

Send order to: Bantam Books, Dept. FN 16, 2451 S. Wolf Rd., Des Plaines, IL 60018
Allow four to six weeks for delivery.

Prices and availability subject to change without notice.   FN 16 9/98

Bestselling Historical Women's Fiction

⚹ IRIS JOHANSEN ⚹

____28855-5 THE WIND DANCER ...$5.99/$6.99

____29968-9 THE TIGER PRINCE ...$6.99/$8.99

____29944-1 THE MAGNIFICENT

ROGUE ....$6.99/$8.99

____29945-X BELOVED SCOUNDREL .$6.99/$8.99

____29946-8 MIDNIGHT WARRIOR ..$6.99/$8.99

____29947-6 DARK RIDER ....$6.99/$8.99

____56990-2 LION'S BRIDE ....$6.99/$8.99

____56991-0 THE UGLY DUCKLING...$6.99/$8.99

____57181-8 LONG AFTER MIDNIGHT.$6.99/$8.99

____57998-3 AND THEN YOU DIE.... $6.99/$8.99

⚹ TERESA MEDEIROS ⚹

____29407-5 HEATHER AND VELVET .$5.99/$7.50

____29409-1 ONCE AN ANGEL .....$5.99/$7.99

____29408-3 A WHISPER OF ROSES .$5.99/$7.99

____56332-7 THIEF OF HEARTS .....$5.50/$6.99

____56333-5 FAIREST OF THEM ALL .$5.99/$7.50

____56334-3 BREATH OF MAGIC ....$5.99/$7.99

____57623-2 SHADOWS AND LACE ...$5.99/$7.99

____57500-7 TOUCH OF ENCHANTMENT.$5.99/$7.99

____57501-5 NOBODY'S DARLING ...$5.99/$7.99
